A TRIANGLE OF LOVERS

MADAME PICARD—The haunting French siren who destroyed everything she loved.

MAJOR WILLIAM FOSTER—A tyrant of stone, he taught his men to be soldiers—even if it killed them.

MARCO SEGRAIN—Gypsy, jewel thief, con-man, circus barker and gigolo—he was expected to die when he joined the Legion. But he learned to be a killer and grew to be a hero.

MARCH OR DIE
The blazing novel of romance
and adventure by Robert Weverka.

Sir Lew Grade
presents
for
Associated General Films
A Dick Richards Film

GENE TERENCE MAX
HACKMAN HILL VON SYDOW

MARCH OR DIE

also starring
IAN HOLM
as
"El Krim"
and
CATHERINE DENEUVE
as
"Simone"

Directed by Dick Richards

Produced by Dick Richards
and
Jerry Bruckheimer

Screenplay by David Zelag Goodman

Story by David Zelag Goodman
and
Dick Richards

Music by Maurice Jarre

A Columbia Pictures Release
from
ITC Entertainment

March
or
Die

Robert Weverka

Based on the Screenplay by
David Zelag Goodman

Screenstory by David Zelag Goodman
and Dick Richards

BANTAM BOOKS
TORONTO · NEW YORK · LONDON

MARCH OR DIE
A Bantam Book / August 1977

ISBN 0-553-11261-9

Published simultaneously in the United States and Canada

Bantam Books are published by Bantam Books, Inc. Its trade-
mark, consisting of the words "Bantam Books" and the por-
trayal of a bantam, is registered in the United States Patent
Office and in other countries. Marca Registrada. Bantam
Books, Inc., 666 Fifth Avenue, New York, New York 10019.

PRINTED IN THE UNITED STATES OF AMERICA

March
or
Die

I

French Morocco, 1918.

Lieutenant Fontaine of the French Foreign Legion studied the eastern horizon for several minutes, noting the shape and curve and dip of each distant sand dune, searching carefully for what might prove to be an Arab sentry, or a tent, or a moving camel. He could see nothing; no movement, no smoke, no fires, no signs of life. But he knew the Arabs were there, and he knew they would be coming; hundreds, maybe thousands of them would come charging across the desert, swords flashing, screaming praises to Allah, the ground trembling under the hooves of their horses and camels.

Behind Fontaine the other legionnaires were moving about quietly, most of them only half-awake. Fires were being started, and the soft clatter of tin cups and coffee pots invaded the early-morning silence. Farther away on the other side of the archaeological excavation, the Arab workmen already had their fires going, and the rhythmic wailing and moaning of their morning prayers drifted softly across the camp.

Fontaine smiled bitterly to himself. Were the workmen praying there would be no attack this morning so they could earn another day's wages? Or were they praying for the death of the legionnaires so they could loot whatever the attackers left of their supplies and

1

equipment? Either way, Allah was going to provide for them. And very likely they all knew the exact time El Krim, the guerrilla leader, was going to make his attack.

"Good morning, lieutenant. Enjoying the sunrise?"

The man walking toward him with a cup of coffee in his hand was Henri Delacorte, the museum curator in charge of the excavation. He was a tall, handsome man with silver-gray hair—a man Fontaine found himself disliking more every day. This morning he was wearing a silk paisley scarf tucked into the collar of his suntan shirt.

"I am not very fond of sunrises, Monsieur Delacorte."

Fontaine lifted his field glasses, this time scanning the dark mountains to the northwest. The sun was now touching their snow-capped, thirteen-thousand-foot peaks. "I am not fond of sunrises, Monsieur Delacorte, because dawn is the Arab's favorite hour for attacking."

Fontaine knew Delacorte did not take his warnings seriously. For three days running, El Krim's men had been observing their encampment. When Fontaine's scouts were patrolling the east or west, a camel rider would suddenly appear in the north or south. Then another would appear in the east or west as the patrols passed.

"Perhaps they're just curious," Delacorte had suggested last night when Fontaine told him what was going on.

"Perhaps," Fontaine said, but he knew better. He had been in the Legion fourteen years now, with every one of those years spent in the mountains or deserts of Morocco. When Arabs were curious, they took one look and moved on. When they were planning an attack, they took many looks, counting soldiers and guns and checking fortifications.

"If I might make a suggestion, lieutenant," Delacorte said now, "wouldn't it be wise for us to have a talk with this El Krim fellow? After all, we do have the sultan's permission to be here. Perhaps if you and

I rode over to his camp and showed him our papers—"

"Monsieur Delacorte, if El Krim attacks, I would suggest that you get rid of those papers as quickly as you can. You will most certainly get special treatment if he finds them in your possession."

Fontaine moved away from the archaeologist cursing the circumstances that had put them all in such an impossible situation. Nobody in Paris, it seemed, was the least bit interested in making inquiries about what was going on in Morocco before they sent people down here. Two archaeologists theorized there was some kind of lost tomb or hidden treasure buried in the desert, and some ninny of an official in Paris said, "Fine, go look for it, and take along a company or two of legionnaires to watch over things." Except they didn't bother to find out that the sultan of Morocco had no control whatsoever over the part of the country where they wanted to dig, and there was nothing the tribal leader, El Krim, would like better than the opportunity to show France and the sultan what he thought of them by wiping out a bunch of infidel trespassers. And from what Fontaine's scouts had determined, the main body of El Krim's warriors was camped only fifteen miles away at the foot of the Atlas Mountains. So it was like climbing over a fence and digging in somebody's backyard. They could dig as long as El Krim permitted it, and then their bodies would be left to the buzzards and jackals, and their heads would be delivered to the gates of the nearest Legion post.

"*Levez-vous! Levez-vous!*" Fontaine shouted as he moved among the tents, waking up his men.

Fontaine knew this would be the day. He had awakened two hours before dawn, that sick feeling deep in his stomach, and for a long time he had lain with his hands behind his head gazing emptily into the darkness. He alternately felt chills, and then a rapid heartbeat, and then difficulty catching his breath. Why? He was not afraid to die. A man expected to die when he joined the Legion. Then why was he reacting so strangely now?

He finally dressed himself and spent the next

hour and a half pacing slowly from one end of the encampment to the other. For a while he had gazed down at the sleeping Arab workmen, feeling bitterness and hatred for them. They were like buzzards and jackals themselves—smiling Judases who would lie, cheat, and steal, and stab any legionnaire in the back for half a sou, and then give thanks to Allah for the opportunity.

On the other hand, he couldn't blame them. They felt the French government was stabbing them in the back, too, and there was probably some truth in it. It never occurred to people like Delacorte and his assistant that the Arabs regarded the desert and anything buried in it as their property.

What had surprised Fontaine was that El Krim had permitted the digging to go on for almost three months without firing a shot or even voicing an objection. But there could be an explanation for it. He might have been curious, wondering what they were digging for, and then waiting to see if they were going to find it. But now it looked as if he had had enough. He was getting impatient, or irritated, or plain infuriated at their squatting under his nose.

In the center of the excavation, a high mound of dirt and boulders rose fifteen feet above the level of the desert. Fontaine climbed to the top and brought his field glasses out again, once more scanning the horizons. With the sky now turning slate-gray, he could see the two-man patrol coming in from the southwest. Both men had their thumbs hooked in their rifle straps, moving steadily, showing no signs of alarm. He couldn't find the other patrol on the opposite side, but he didn't worry about it yet. Passing between the long, rolling sand dunes, they could easily be blocked from view for lengthy periods.

Then, to the northeast, he saw the first Arab come into view. As he moved the glasses slowly across a distant dune, the form suddenly appeared, wobbling for a moment as the camel came up a steep slope, and stopped on the crest of the dune. Then a second and a third joined the first one, and all three of the burnoose-clad riders sat perfectly still, seeming to gaze directly back into Fontaine's eyes.

He returned the glasses to the case and gazed around at the small camp. How long would it be? An hour? Two hours? He didn't have the slightest doubt that they would all be dead before sunset. So their duty was to kill as many Arabs as possible before they died.

The men were all veterans, and he had no doubts about how they would handle themselves. But exposed as they were in the middle of the desert, they would have little chance against such overwhelming odds.

"Sergeant!"

"Yes, lieutenant!" the man said and hurried over. He was still buttoning his pants.

"See that every man has one hundred rounds of ammunition. And each man is to have a double ration of breakfast. Then we will assume battle formation on the north and west perimeters."

"Yes, lieutenant. Do you think they're coming, sir?"

Fontaine was certain they were coming. But saying so would sound foolish. "I don't know, sergeant."

At noon the dispatch rider arrived from Bousaada. On all four sides there were Arab sentries; two or three men sitting on camels, staring silently at the small cluster of legionnaires. But they made no effort to stop the courier. The rider was a spahi cavalryman, and he had a look of fear on his face when he saluted Fontaine and handed over his message.

"The German army has agreed to armistice terms," the dispatch read; "All hostilities will cease at eleven A.M., 11 November 1918. Congratulations to all French army units. We are victorious!"

Fontaine handed the message to Delacorte and looked out across the desert to the north, where a great cloud of dust was beginning to form. "What is the date today, sergeant?"

"The eleventh of November, sir."

Fontaine nodded, half-smiling at the irony of it.

"The war in Europe has ended, sergeant. Inform the men."

It was good news about other people, delivered to doomed men. There were no shouts or cries of joy. Some of the men, perhaps those with relatives still in France, showed some satisfaction. Others nodded and kept their eyes fixed on the distant dust cloud, while the German legionnaires among them frowned, probably wondering if they would have a homeland anymore.

Fontaine had avoided Henri Delacorte as much as he could this morning. The curator had come looking for him several times, complaining about the Arab workmen. They were all slacking off, spending most of their time staring off at the desert.

"Don't worry about it," Fontaine told him, "They'll be leaving shortly."

"Then they won't be paid."

Fontaine had smiled at that and moved away. But now Delacorte seemed to be getting the picture. He, too, was frowning off at the dust cloud.

"Is the wind causing that, lieutenant?" he asked.

"I'm more inclined to think it is El Krim, Monsieur Delacorte."

The cloud was growing broader, spreading to the north and west. Then the first of the camel riders came into view at the top of a distant slope.

"If you and your assistant would prefer to make a run for it, monsieur, I would advise you to get on camels and leave as quickly as possible."

They could hear it now, the distant shouts and the low rumble of galloping hooves.

"My God!" Delacorte breathed as he stared at the growing mass. He looked over at his gaping assistant and then turned back to Fontaine. "If we go, do you think we could make it?"

"No," Fontaine said. He moved over to where the soldiers were forming a perimeter. "First company, front rank," he commanded. "Second company, rear."

The men moved sharply into position, a straight line with those in front kneeling. The sergeant took a position at the far end. Including Fontaine, there were fifty-two men.

The ground was beginning to vibrate now. Coming toward them in a broad line were about five hundred camels and horses. Behind them were at least seven hundred men on foot, the skirts of their djellabas flying, their long swords flashing in the sun. Twenty-five to one, Fontaine reflected as the first distant pops of rifle fire sent pieces of lead skipping off the sand and whispering through the air overhead.

Fontaine spread his legs, standing easily, his hands behind his back, feeling a trickle of perspiration slide down his ribs. "First rank . . . Fire!"

A dozen camels went down, their riders sprawling into the sand. But the Arab ranks quickly closed, the charging line once again solid.

"Second rank . . . Fire!"

Again camels and Arabs tumbled, and again there was no visible thinning of their forces. Seven legionnaires were already hit.

"Machine gun, commence firing!" Fontaine ordered. "Rifles, continuous fire!"

It was all so stupid, Fontaine thought bitterly. They were close enough now, and he raised his pistol, methodically aiming, shooting, aiming again, until the chamber was empty. There was no visible effect from his bullets flying into the onrushing mass. "Fix bayonets!" he ordered as he reloaded.

The charging camels and horsemen were almost on them now. The flank riders were circling broadly to the side, firing at the spahis who had taken random positions in the excavation.

His pistol loaded, Fontaine raised it just in time as a camel bore down on him, its rider wielding a long straight sword. Fontaine fired and the man disappeared as the camel thundered past.

The French Foreign Legion is the finest army in the world. The words tumbled through Fontaine's mind as he fired again and again. *A legionnaire never flinches in the face of battle. A legionnaire is fearless, and no matter what the odds against him, a legion-*

*naire will always emerge victorious. A legionnaire does
his duty.*

The situation was hopeless. The mass of Arabs
was now upon them, their swords flashing, hacking
right and left at their victims. Fontaine whirled, firing as rapidly as he could in the midst of the carnage;
at the same time dodging and twisting, trying to keep
away from the flailing swords. Then he was down,
sprawling to his hands and knees as he tripped over
the body of a fallen legionnaire. He scrambled to the
side, quickly reloading in the forest of twisting hooves
and legs. He shot one and then another of the screaming riders, and then as he came up and swung around,
he caught only a quick glimpse of the heavy blade that
struck solidly into the left side of his face.

He was down again, this time across the body of
a fallen Arab. He groped feebly to pull himself up.
The left side of his face was numb, and for a minute he
could hear nothing but a steady ringing sound. But
there was still movement around him. He lay still,
breathing deeply, the pain now burning across his
head. He twisted and looked behind him.

He could see with only one eye. The other was
sticky with blood, and the lid would not open.

The Arabs had now moved on to the excavation, screaming down into it, some of them laughing as
they brandished rifles and swords over their heads.
Fontaine watched for a minute and then inched himself forward across the sand. Six feet ahead was a
latrine ditch, with wooden planks covering part of it.
He kept moving, knowing his chances were slim, but
hoping that whatever was in the excavation would keep
everybody's attention for a minute more.

He made it. He slid into the shallow trench and
then forced himself forward, squeezing under the
planks. He closed his eyes and gasped for breath, willing himself not to drop into unconsciousness.

Where the studding held the planks above the
ground, a narrow crack gave him a partial view of
the excavation area. Fontaine lifted his head against
the planks and squinted out. Then he felt a cold chill
go through his body.

Henri Delacorte was being dragged feet-first out of a deep excavation trench. Most of his clothing had been torn off, and he was kicking and screaming as they pulled him up and stretched him across the saddle of a camel.

Then Fontaine saw the other man—Delacorte's assistant. He was already stripped naked and stretched across the back of a horse, his head on one side, his legs on the other, his wrists and ankles tied underneath.

Just beyond, El Krim was watching from the saddle of a big white horse. "Allah!" he shouted and lifted his rifle high in the air.

"Allah! Allah! Allah!" his men answered.

Fontaine eased his head into the muck and closed his eyes. He should have warned Delacorte and his assistant. He should have given them pistols to kill themselves.

But it was all so stupid, Fontaine told himself. *The French government was stupid, the archaeologists were stupid for wanting to come here, and the Legion was stupid to go along with it.*

The blood from his cheek oozed slowly into the mud, and Fontaine finally lost consciousness.

II

The streets of Paris were mobbed. Flags waved from every window; British flags, American flags, Belgian, Dutch, Canadian, Australian—flags from every nation whose valiant young men had come to France to defeat the *Boches*. Mostly they were the French tricolor, and the Parisians waved them proudly and exuberantly.

On every street, girls rushed out to hug and kiss the returning heroes, and as the grinning soldiers marched past, shopkeepers handed them glasses and bottles and cups and carafes of wine and cognac and champagne, and for days "The Marseillaise," "God Save the King," and "The Star Spangled Banner" resounded through the city. Long live France! Long live England and America! After four bitter years of fighting, the *Boches* had been defeated.

People smiled and waved and threw flowers along the railroad tracks. Soldiers hanging from the train windows grinned and shouted and waved back as the packed railroad cars crept slowly into the city. The war was over! The bloodiest, most devastating war in modern history was over, and the world was safe for democracy, freedom, equality, and liberty. *Vive la victoire!*

Major William Sherman Foster of the French Foreign Legion stood silently at the window of his compartment, feeling little emotion as he gazed out at the welcoming crowds. Foster was in his early forties; a stocky, muscular man whose chiseled features and stone-gray eyes reflected twenty-three years of disciplined military life.

The people of Paris and the surrounding countryside were all strange and foreign to him; a world he had neither seen nor thought about in the past four years, and a part of civilization he knew little about and had no interest in. They were farmers and merchants and shopkeepers, and he was a soldier. He knew nothing of their thoughts and hopes and dreams, and they knew nothing of his. And while they were celebrating what they called victory, they had no idea of what a wholesale disaster the past four years had been.

It had not been a war; a military battle of trained and disciplined soldiers fighting against an equally well-disciplined army. It had been a collection of buffoons and inept dilettantes with swagger sticks overseeing the slaughter of millions of men who had no business wearing military uniforms or handling deadly weapons. And trapped in the idiocy had been thousands of legionnaires who were always ordered to do the wrong thing at the wrong time and who were too well disciplined and had too strong a sense of duty to refuse the orders.

So be it, Foster thought. As the Arabs said, "It is so written." And twenty-three years ago, when he chose a military career, he had no illusions about who ultimately gave the orders. It was always the politicians, and they were always passed on by the politician-generals. It would always be that way, and there was nothing Foster could do to change it.

"Triand!" he called out as the train moved into the station and the brakes began to groan and squeal.

"Oui, mon commandant!"

The man answering the call was Sergeant Michael Triand, a thirty-year veteran of the Legion. He was a short, burly man, his face creased and hard from long years of service in Algeria and Morocco.

"The men will form ranks on the platform immediately outside the railroad cars, sergeant. All of them."

"The wounded too, sir?"

"All of them, sergeant."

"*Oui, mon commandant.*"

When the train finally stopped, Foster closed the curtains of the compartment and waited five minutes before striding through the passageway and out to the platform. The station was jammed with people; friends and family members rushing to greet the outpouring of returning soldiers. It was apparent that the regular-army men had no instructions for an orderly debarkation. They were scattering pell-mell over the platform, shouting, laughing, embracing those who had come to meet them. In marked contrast, the legionnaires had formed ranks, partially obstructing the heavy flow of traffic. Among them were a good many wounded; heads bandaged, arms in slings, men on crutches, others being supported by their comrades.

"Attention!" the sergeant bawled out, and the men stiffened and fixed their eyes forward.

It was a small thing, but Foster wanted them to be noticed, and for it to be apparent that they were different from the others. He did not want their wounded to be hidden or spirited off on some railroad siding. He wanted the Parisians and the other servicemen to see what real soldiers looked like.

The sergeant's abrupt call to attention brought a sudden silence to the station. Other soldiers turned uncertainly, and a band near the stairs stopped playing. Foster marched to the front of the formation and stood in silence for another full minute.

"You have all fought well," he finally said, his commanding voice echoing through the station. "You have done your duty, and you have been victorious. There will be a forty-eight-hour leave, and then you will all report to the Legion barracks for new assignment." He paused, gazing silently at the weary, battle-scarred faces and broken bodies. The small company represented only one-fifth of the men he had taken to the front four years earlier. He felt anger and bitterness when he remembered those who would not be coming back. Then he stiffened and snapped the men a quick salute. "Company, dismissed!"

Outside the station, a hundred people were waiting for taxis, and Foster had to walk three blocks before he found an empty one. "Do you know where the Americans are assembling their dead bodies for shipment home?" he asked the driver.

"Oui, monsieur," the man said and Foster climbed in.

His orders called for him to report to the Élysée Palace at two o'clock, but it was only a little after one now, and Foster relaxed, gazing silently out the window as the driver picked his way through the crowded streets.

Four years had passed since he had been in Paris. That was in October of 1914, when his regiment was being rushed to the front from Morocco. The city looked grim and frightened then. Now it seemed gay and confident, almost arrogant over being spared from the destruction of German guns.

It was strange to see so many people wearing civilian clothes, to see streets and shops, people sipping drinks in outdoor cafés. He had almost forgotten such things existed. But no doubt he would be on his way to some remote military post in a few days, and he would soon forget such things again.

When he looked back on his life, Foster found it hard to remember when he was not a soldier. At the age of fourteen, when he was growing up in Pittsburgh, he had made a firm decision to go to West Point and become an officer in the United States Army. He could not recall ever having considered any other career.

He had graduated from West Point at the top of his class. "An officer destined to a great career in the United States Army," General Hayford had said at the commencement exercises. "A young man whose dedication and perseverance should be an example to all his classmates and to all future cadets at the Academy. Lieutenant William Sherman Foster, the Academy is proud of you, and knows that you will carry on the great traditions of its many illustrious graduates."

Foster had carried on those great traditions for exactly eleven months and nine days. And then he had stood face-to-face with Colonel Theodore Roosevelt—a politician who had never worn a uniform until ninety days earlier—and said, "With all due respect, colonel, a direct assault on the Spanish fortified positions would be ridiculous and would unnecessarily result in extremely high casualties." At noon the next day, he was ordered out of Cuba, and a week later he received orders assigning him to duty as a procurement officer in Washington, D.C. Foster had resigned his commission three days later. At least he submitted his resignation—whether or not it was accepted he never knew, because the day after he handed it in, he was on a ship bound for France. At first he petitioned for a new assignment, requesting cavalry duty in the Arizona Territory, or the Philippines, or China, or anywhere else he might see some action. When that was denied, he was given permission to talk to the colonel about it, and it was during that two-minute interview that he decided to join the French Foreign Legion.

"Your orders are to report to Washington, D.C., lieutenant. Why do you question them?"

"I question them, sir, because I am trained to be a soldier, and I am a good one. I think the army needs good officers in places where there is likely to be trouble."

"Part of being a good soldier is obeying orders, Lieutenant Foster."

"Yes, sir," Foster said, knowing that part of being a colonel and being promoted to general meant not doing any favors for young lieutenants who had questioned the wisdom of politician-soldiers.

"General Meyers has requested a young officer for his staff in Washington, D.C., lieutenant. I think you are suited for the job and that you will find it rewarding. That will be all, lieutenant."

"Yes, sir. Thank you, sir."

Foster sometimes marveled at his own audacity and impertinence, and at the apparent indifference with which the United States Army let him go. If one of his legionnaire lieutenants handed in a resignation and jumped on a ship, Foster would personally chase him halfway around the world and bring him back in irons. But he hadn't heard a word from the U.S. Army. Three weeks later, with forty other recruits, he was crammed into the dirty hold of a small steamship crossing the Mediterranean from Marseilles to Oran.

Foster never did know what the colonel in the Legion recruiting office thought about getting a young West Point graduate. Foster had volunteered the information, but it was the Legion's policy to ask no questions. The colonel had only stared at him for a minute and then pushed the gray enlistment form across the desk. "If you can prove that you have been an officer in the army of your own country, you will begin as a probationary corporal, *mon enfant*. Otherwise—" With that he smiled and shrugged his shoulders.

"I will begin as a recruit, *mon commandant*."

"Very well. Then take these papers to your hotel and sleep on it. Tomorrow, if you are still interested in being a legionnaire, we will accept your enlistment."

Foster smiled as he thought back on that day. He had often wondered how many young men did not return the next morning. As for himself, the delay had angered him more than anything, and not having a hotel room, he had walked the streets of Paris all night, hating all of it. And then he had spent an hour in the room of a prostitute, too distracted to get his money's worth.

The Legion had not turned out to be as exciting and adventurous as the posters promised, and in the first year he saw no action at all. But he thrived on the spartan life; the long desert marches, the lonely garrison duty, and the chance to demonstrate that he was a tougher and more durable soldier than his fellow recruits. After four years, he was made a sergeant; and three years later, after a hundred fifty-seven men died in the siege of Dziona, he was cited for extraordinary service and promoted to lieutenant.

He was a captain, stationed in Boudenib, when the war broke out in Europe. When he was ordered to return to France, he anticipated a quick and decisive victory over the Germans. There was no army in the world as tough and well trained as the French Foreign Legion, and nobody in the world would be fool enough not to give them a free rein in leading the battle against the invaders.

But Foster soon discovered that the world was full of fools. He was ordered to dig trenches and build useless fortifications, and then they sat down and waited. They waited for German artillery to cut them to shreds, and they waited for sickness and disease, and they waited for poison gas to drift into their positions. And when they finally attacked, they moved forward like a huge, fat, frightened animal, hoping that enough of them would live long enough to capture a hundred yards of territory. And then once a month the generals with their swagger sticks and bellies full of champagne ventured cautiously to the front and told them all they were brave soldiers and doing a wonderful job.

And finally the Americans came. They came with their pink faces and clean uniforms and their fine young officers who had yet to see a live bullet or a piece of searing-hot shrapnel, or a soldier trying to stuff his guts back into his belly. And they were told to dig trenches and sit in them until the Germans ran out of ammunition or got tired of killing people.

So it was written, as the Arabs said. But to Foster it seemed a miracle that the war ever ended—much less that it had been won by the Allies—and he had begun to wonder if the whole thing was no more than a deliberate plan by both sides to annihilate all the able-bodied men in the world. He also wondered where all the generals and colonels in the world learned how to fight a war. From what he had witnessed, their education came from pushing salt- and pepper-shakers back and forth across linen tablecloths.

They were somewhere on the outskirts of town when the taxi driver finally stopped the car. The place looked like a park or an old cemetery, with thousands of pine-box caskets spread across several acres. American army trucks were delivering more caskets, while another line of trucks was loading up to carry them away. A lieutenant standing next to a truck with several file cabinets seemed to be in charge of things. Foster told the driver to wait, and he threaded his way through the crowd of loitering soldiers.

"Do you have the body of a man named Paul Chase?" he asked the man.

The lieutenant handed some papers to a waiting truck driver and gave Foster a sour look as he turned away. "Damned if I know, pal."

"Lieutenant!" Foster commanded.

The man had turned to rummage through the drawer of a file cabinet. He looked up sharply.

"I want to know if you have the body of Colonel Paul Chase of the United States Army!"

A dozen soldiers were staring now, and the lieutenant gazed indecisively at him. "I'll take a look, major."

"I will appreciate that, lieutenant."

"Section E, number eighty-four," the lieutenant said after he shuffled through a stack of forms. "Sergeant, show the major where it is."

Foster followed the sergeant to a far corner of the area where the casket was resting on top of two others. An American flag was draped over the stack.

Foster drew the flag back and looked off to where a man was leaning against a tree, supposedly standing guard. "Soldier! Bring me your bayonet!"

The man handed over his bayonet, and Foster forced it under the lid of the coffin.

"Hey, for chrissake, you can't do that!"

Foster ignored him. He pried the lid open a half-inch, then shifted the blade and levered it free.

"Jesus, are you some kind of—?"

Foster glared coldly at the sergeant and the wide-eyed soldier. They both blinked for a minute and backed away. "Excuse me, sir," the sergeant said.

Foster was not certain why he had a compulsion to look at the body. Paul Chase had been his only fond memory of West Point and his brief career in the United States Army. Three months ago he had received a note from Chase telling him he was in France, and

then they had gotten messages back and forth agreeing
to meet in Paris when the war was over. But then
Foster's last message had been returned with a note
scrawled across the side: "Colonel Chase was killed
in Meuse-Argonne, 11–2–18."

The body was wrapped loosely in some kind of
oiled material. Foster drew the folds away from the
head and gazed silently at it, his throat tightening. It
looked stiff; the skin drawn tightly across the bones,
and the mouth partially open. But it was Paul Chase.

"I should be in there instead of you," Foster
told him silently. "You had a home and a future, and
I'm tired. So you're going to Arlington to rest, and I'm
going back to the desert and more death."

The tears were beginning to form in his eyes, and
he finally leaned forward and kissed both of the waxy
cheeks. Then he replaced the folds. After he set the
top of the coffin back in position, he stepped back and
saluted.

Paul Chase was the last thread connecting him to
anyplace he might have called home. Now the thread
was broken. The only place he could call home now
was the Sahara Desert.

III

The train trip from Cannes to Paris had taken all night and most of the following day. For hours at a time they had stopped on sidings while troop trains sped south, returning victorious soldiers to their homes. Then, each time they started moving again, the train had crept along, traveling no more than an hour or two before it stopped at another small town to drop off freight cars.

The two police inspectors were bored and exhausted by the endless tedium. They sat in separate seats, one ahead of the other, their manacled prisoner beside the man in the rear. Of the three men, only the prisoner seemed to be enjoying the trip. He was a dark, handsome man, probably in his early thirties. He was wearing a dinner jacket and an expensive silk shirt, but his collar was now open. His dark eyes seemed to take increasing pleasure in the landscape as the train moved at a snail's pace into the suburbs of Paris.

One might have guessed him to be a professional man of some kind—perhaps in some not-quite-respectable occupation—a gambler, an entertainer, perhaps an overly suave *maitre d'* in an expensive restaurant.

Although the arrest warrants carried the name Marco LeClerc, alias Marco DeMarot, Anton Dozier and Jean-Paul Delattre, his real name was Marco Segrain. By lineage he was half-gypsy, and under various names he was a citizen of Spain, France, England, Italy, Switzerland and Rumania; and he was fluent in all of those languages. By profession he was a jewel

thief, swindler, confidence man, circus barker, wood-
cutter, tinker, and lady's companion; and as often as
not, he practiced two or three of these at the same
time in order to assure his survival. At the moment he
was a prisoner, but it was a state of affairs not entirely
new to him. It was also one that he did not expect to
last long.

The appearance of the two inspectors had come as
a surprise and at an unfortunate time for Marco. He
was just returning from a cocktail party on the yacht
of a Greek banker when he found the two dumpy-
looking men awaiting him in the lobby of the hotel.
It was unfortunate because the charming and slightly
inebriated English lady he was escorting home was
wearing a dazzling diamond pendant worth at least
100,000 francs.

The lady had been much distressed by the rude-
ness and stupidity of the policemen. She indignantly
advised them that it was clearly a case of mistaken
identity, Monsieur Jean-Paul Delattre could not possibly be the criminal they were seeking. She would
inform the British consul of the incident as quickly as
she could ring him up. Marco had assured her that
she was quite correct in her assessment of the situation,
but he graciously consented to accompany the two men
to the office of the Prefecture of Police, from which
he promised to return within the hour.

Marco smiled to himself now as he reflected on
the unfortunate lady's frustrations. Cannes was a lonely
place for middle-aged ladies whose husbands were
off fighting the Germans, and no doubt she had passed
the remainder of the evening listening anxiously for his
soft knock on her door.

He had no intention of taking her pendant that
night. He would have insisted that she put it in a safe
place; some obscure drawer, or powder box, or the
toe of a shoe. Such places were far safer than the hotel
safe. Thievery among hotel employees was notorious
in the South of France, and even the managers had
been known to flee with the valuable jewels of guests.
Then, perhaps three or four nights later, he would have
returned by way of a window, or by picking the lock

of her door, and he would have relieved the lady of any further necessity to look for hiding places.

What had surprised Marco about his arrest was that he could hardly remember the crime for which the warrant had been issued. It was the theft of twenty-four pearl necklaces from a Parisian jeweler.

"Madame Chardonet? I have never heard of such a lady," he told the policeman. "And I have not been in Paris since the beginning of the war."

"That is exactly when it happened," one of the inspectors said as he filled out papers in the prefecture office. "She gave us a positive identification last week."

And then Marco had vaguely recalled the circumstances. He had admired the lady's pearls while visiting an art show, and she had informed him that her husband was a dealer. So Marco had cultivated a friendship and visited the lady's boudoir on several occasions. But altogether it had been a dull affair, and as he departed one afternoon, he simply picked up and carried off a package that had been left in the foyer of her apartment. In such circumstances, a discreet lady usually did not inform her husband of any visitors she might have entertained during the day. But after four years, Madame Chardonet must have grown bitter and decided Marco was not going to return.

C'est la vie. And what had he done with the pearls? He couldn't remember. Perhaps that had been how he financed his way to Cannes when the war started.

It would not have been difficult for him to escape when the two policemen took him to the railroad station the next night. He was agile enough to have jumped from the police car, or broken away in the crowded station, and have returned to the lovely lady's hotel to pick up the sparklers. But he had grown tired of the Riviera. With the war over, he was looking forward to seeing Paris and old friends again. So he had protested vigorously over the arrest, and then, with his manacled wrists between his legs and secured to a steel brace under the seat, he had made himself as comfortable as possible and enjoyed the passing scenery. Except for the physical discomfort and the dullness of his two companions, it was a pleasant enough journey. But now, with the station only minutes away, Marco glanced thoughtfully down the aisle and considered the possibilities of escape.

The car was crowded. While the victorious soldiers were traveling south, returning to their homes, an equal number of civilians appeared to be returning to Paris now that it was safe. Mostly they were women and children and old men, and the aisle was cluttered with boxes and bags and battered suitcases, making it almost impossible for the conductor to make his way through. Marco studied all this, and the stacks of luggage and boxes in the small alcove at the front of the car. There would be a great deal of confusion when the train stopped in the station. People would be anxious to find their bags and get out, and with no porters to help them, there would be a great tangle of bodies near the door. That certainly might provide the opportunity. After that, the station would also be crowded, but no doubt there would be a great many soldiers and policemen about.

The car suddenly darkened as they left the sunlight and passed into the shadowy interior of the station. People began to rise, gathering their things, and the train vibrated and squealed as the brakes were applied. The policeman next to Marco put his newspaper aside. He fished in a pocket, brought out his keys, and then shook his sleeping comrade in the seat ahead. After he released the handcuffs anchoring Marco to the seat, he rose and grunted, motioning Marco to hurry. Apparently he hoped to beat the crowd out the door. The other policeman moved ahead, keeping Marco sandwiched between the two of them.

"Excuse us, please. Excuse me. Let us through, please."

Marco waited until they had squeezed almost out of the luggage room. Then he hesitated, looking at the floor as if being careful not to trip over something. By then the first policeman was starting down the stairs behind several other people. Marco quickly turned, giving the policeman behind him a hard shove.

At the side, suitcases, duffel bags and boxes were piled almost to the ceiling. Marco yanked at a heavy bag in the middle of the pile, triggering an avalanche into the already congested aisle. Moving quickly forward, he planted his foot between the shoulder blades of the policeman on the steps and sent him sprawling into the crowd waiting below.

Screams and angry shouts were suddenly coming from all directions. Behind him, people were half-buried under the luggage. In front, the policeman had crashed into three or four other people, carrying them down the steps and into a tangled heap on the floor of the station.

"Be careful, monsieur!" a man yelled at him.

Marco smiled at him and moved quickly down the steps, squeezing past the crowd. Then he dropped to his hands and knees and scrambled under the railroad car. It was awkward crawling past the tracks with his wrists handcuffed, but he made it. A police whistle sounded as he came to his feet and ran along the other side. More whistles sounded, and he heard one of the inspectors shouting, saying he had gone under the train.

Another train was parked on the next track, and Marco quickly dropped again and scrambled under. When he came up, a string of passenger cars loaded with soldiers was moving past, slowly gathering speed as it headed out of the station. Marco jogged alongside until the steps at the end of a car were passing by. He grabbed the railing with both hands and jumped up, quickly pressing himself into the recessed area in front of the closed door. Then, gasping to catch his breath, he leaned out far enough to see behind him. Then he grinned. The two inspectors were standing on the empty tracks, staring at the departing caboose.

A military band was playing in front of the Élysée Palace, and the crowds of celebrating people had brought traffic to a standstill. Foster got out of the taxi and walked the last block to where Triand was waiting for him.

"I'm afraid you may be a little late, sir," the sergeant said.

Foster smiled as they went up the steps. "I doubt if anybody is on time today, sergeant."

Inside the palace, it was as crowded as the streets were. It looked as if every general from every army of the Allied forces was there; each looking as if he had personally won the war.

"Foster, is that you?"

Foster turned, frowning at the man who had grabbed his arm. It was an American brigadier general.

"Don't you remember me? Palmer. Arthur Palmer."

Foster remembered and stared at the man with surprise. At West Point, Arthur Palmer had a hard time finding where the bathroom was, and he had never managed to reassemble a rifle so that it would fire. But his father was a wealthy New York stockbroker, and a lot of his clients were retired generals.

"How are you, Palmer?" Foster said.

"Wonderful, wonderful. I see you're a major now."

"That's right," Foster nodded, "I guess promotions come a little slower in the Legion than they do in the U.S. Army."

"What's the Legion really like?" Palmer asked, "Is it as tough as they say?"

"No, it's about the same as West Point. Football games, Saturday-night dances. I'm sorry, general, but I've got to go."

Triand was waiting at the stairs for him. They went up two at a time, and then hurried along the corridor to the minister's office. "Christ, I'd like to have that guy in Africa for a while," Foster muttered. "As a recruit."

Two Legion colonels were waiting in the anteroom, standing in a far corner, smoking and talking in low voices. Foster and Triand saluted.

"Hello, Foster. How are you?"

Colonel Dechamps, the older of the two, smiled and moved across the room to shake hands.

"I'm fine, sir. I hope you are well."

The other man was Colonel Lamont, an officer

Foster had served under while he was a lieutenant in Algeria. He was a tough desert veteran with the same feelings about the war as Foster. He nodded, giving Foster a faintly rueful smile that suggested that he was not happy about what was going to happen in the minister's office.

"I'm happy to see you survived, Foster."

"Thank you, sir. I'm happy to see anybody survived."

A male secretary came out of the minister's office and held the door open. "Please come in, gentlemen."

The three officers filed in.

The minister was a large, jowly man—wearing a silk shirt with a little French flag holding his tie. His name was Chambord, and Foster had heard rumors that he made a great deal of money handling contracts for war materiel. He smiled and leaned across his ornate desk to shake hands.

It was the other man who gave Foster a feeling of uneasiness. He was introduced as Francois Marneau, the head of the North African Department of the Louvre Museum, and it was his manner more than his appearance that disturbed Foster.

In Africa, Foster had come across a good many archaeologists and anthropologists and university experts. Some were intelligent men who knew their fields, and also had some respect for other people's knowledge. Others, because they knew something about ancient pots and bones and petrified camel dung, felt nobody could give them any advice about anything. Foster suspected that Marneau was the second type. He was a tall, distinguished-looking man with an air of unshakable self-confidence about him. He looked bored as he half-rose to shake Foster's hand.

"Gentlemen," Chambord said when they were all seated, "I presume you have all read this report concerning the Arab attack that took place on an excavation site in Morocco three days ago."

They all had. Foster had received a copy just before he boarded the train coming back from the front. But the report was sketchy, apparently coming from a friendly Arab who happened to ride past the site the day after the battle.

Chambord gazed irritably at the paper and then set it aside. "We have fought the Germans for four bloody years, and we finally have peace. We have defeated one of the greatest armies ever assembled in the world. And now we have this!" He pushed the report aside with disgust. "After we have humbled the entire German empire, we now sustain a defeat by a bunch of ragged Arabs. Gentlemen, it is embarrassing and humiliating."

About fifty men had been killed, and Chambord was making it sound as though the Arabs had just marched into Paris. It was such nonsense that Foster found so ridiculous in politicians.

"Colonel Dechamps, this report states only that the attack took place at an excavation site in Morocco. *Where* in Morocco?"

"The one at Bousaada, sir."

"Excuse me, sir," Lamont quickly corrected. "The excavation is at a place called Erfoud."

The minister looked from one colonel to the other, as if doubting the competence of both of them. "For God's sake, doesn't anybody know what's going on down there?"

"I'm sorry, sir," Dechamps said. "The report was filed in Bousaada, as I understand. I assumed the excavation was nearby."

Chambord sighed heavily. "Very well. Wherever the place is, we do not want something like this to happen again. Monsieur Marneau wishes to have the excavation reopened and digging resumed as quickly as possible. However, I do not want . . ."

"Excuse me, sir," Foster said. "May I ask a question?"

The minister frowned, not accustomed to being interrupted. "Very well, major."

"It was my understanding that the excavation at Erfoud was closed when the war began—the reason being that we did not have enough legionnaires left in Morocco to protect it. When was it reopened?"

The man from the Louvre gave Foster an impatient glance. "It was reopened in September, major."

"Why?"

Marneau looked surprised by the question. "Why? Because I wanted it reopened. I sensed that the war was coming to an end shortly, and I reasoned that—"

"I am glad you sensed the end of the war, Monsieur Marneau," Foster interrupted. "We were not so perceptive at the front."

Marneau gave him a cool look and turned back to the minister. "The British Museum resumed its excavations in Egypt, and I didn't see any reason why we couldn't do the same in Morocco." He smiled at the two colonels, ignoring Foster. "I think you gentlemen should appreciate that in addition to the prestige and cultural benefits which will accrue to France, there is a great deal of money at stake in projects such as this. I am quite certain that our diggings in Morocco—and particularly those at Erfoud—will yield treasures worth many millions. That is why I ordered the resumption of digging in September, and that is why I am going to personally supervise the present expedition."

"Do you think the treasure is worth the lives of fifty-two legionnaires and your two curators, Monsieur Marneau?" Foster asked.

Colonel Dechamps gave Foster a hard look, but Marneau wasn't bothered by the question. "That is a price, major," he said with a bland smile. "But the treasure at Erfoud may be priceless."

"Major Foster," the minister said, "we all appreciate your dedication to the Legion. However, the decision has already been made." He turned to Marneau. "Just exactly what is it that you expect to find at Erfoud, Marneau?"

Marneau smiled, as if about to reveal a dramatic secret. "A city, gentlemen, which has been buried beneath the desert sands for almost three thousand years. A city where the Berber Joan of Arc is buried. The Red Angel of the Desert, the Berbers call her. And

buried with her is an incalculable fortune in gold and
jewels salvaged from the original Berber culture and
captured from the Phoenicians. The treasure at Erfoud,
gentlemen, could be worth far more than what France
has just spent on this war."

Foster clamped his jaws tight, cautioning himself
to be quiet. But he wondered how much value Marneau put on each soldier who had just died in the war.

"Are you certain the treasure is there?" Chambord asked.

"I can guarantee it, gentlemen. I am absolutely
certain. Finding it now is only a matter of painstaking
excavation and proper protection." Marneau looked at
Foster. "Are you familiar with the Arab leader, El
Krim, major?"

"Yes," Foster said.

"Do you think you can control him?"

"No."

It was a simple answer to a stupid question, and
everybody in the room seemed to be surprised by
Foster's answer except Colonel Lamont. If the entire
French army marched into Morocco, the soldiers might
be able to squeeze El Krim into a corner—but asking
if Foster could control him with the number of men
normally in his command was preposterous.

"Major Foster is quite right, Monsieur Marneau,"
Lamont said. "Nobody will ever control El Krim. I
take it the question you meant to ask is—Can Major
Foster secure the excavation site from El Krim's attack?"

"Of course," Marneau smiled. "I certainly don't
expect you to annihilate the poor beggar and all his
people."

It seemed clear that Foster's new assignment was
to guard Marneau and his party while they dug for
treasure at Erfoud. It didn't surprise Foster, but it
didn't please him either. He especially didn't like the
idea of Marneau's being the one he was supposed to
protect. Marneau did not look like the kind of man
who would adapt well to the desert.

"How many men will be available for the duty?"
Foster asked.

"As many as we can spare," Dechamps answered. "I'd say about two hundred."

"Veterans?"

"About a hundred veterans. I'm afraid we're going to have to rely on new recruits for the rest." Dechamps suddenly smiled and came to his feet. "Monsieur Marneau, I don't think we could find a better man than Major Foster to look after you in Morocco. And major, I am sure you will do a good job of it down there. Your orders are waiting in my office."

"Yes, sir," Foster said automatically. But the thought of two hundred men—half of them new recruits—camped in the middle of El Krim's desert, gave him a sick feeling. If the man from the Louvre had any sense, he would stay home and send several expendable assistants to do the work for him.

It was a small circus, the kind that traveled the countryside performing in villages and hamlets through the summer. In the winter they camped in the suburbs of Paris, opening on weekends only and giving private shows by special arrangement. Altogether there were no more than fifty members in the troupe, and most of those were gypsies. The big top was not very big, and by and large what profits the troupe earned came from the carnie and sideshow booths, along with some quick-change artistry and selective pickpocketing.

There was no performance tonight. The booths were dark, the animals all caged and locked. The only light came from the main tent and the six or seven colorfully decorated gypsy wagons parked alongside.

Marco moved quietly through the shadows, past the lion cages and the rows of shabby booths, until he could see through the door of the tent. Only a few of the lights were burning inside; ten or twelve of the performers standing around, casually practicing their routines. Marco watched, studying the people, and then he smiled broadly. To the side, near the empty stands, Georges Michaud was juggling dumbbells, apparently trying something new by the clumsy way he was handling them.

Marco slipped through the door and moved

quickly around behind the stands. When he was opposite the juggler, he hissed softly through the wooden
bleachers. "Georges!"

The dumbbells all clattered to the ground and the
man gaped at him. "Marco! What the—?"

"Shhhhh!" Marco hissed, and motioned him behind the stands. "I don't want Mama to see me like
this." He grinned and showed the handcuffs.

Georges glanced at the other performers and hus-
tled him back through the shadows toward the door.
"She might be very happy to see you like that. She
could lock you up in her wagon and know where you
are once in a while."

The wagon Georges took him into was crowded
with gypsies, and a rousing cry greeted Marco when he
entered. Marco had not seen many of them since he
left Spain twelve years before, and there was ten minutes of tears and laughter and embracing before he
finished greeting everyone. Hugo, the strongman,
brought out a pair of cutters and quickly snipped Marco's handcuffs, and then a wineskin was passed around.

Apparently the gathering had been a "welcome
home" party for a young man named Marcel who was
wearing a French army uniform with rows of medals
across his chest. After the wine was passed, everybody
settled back and waited for Marcel to continue his
story.

Marco had known Marcel only slightly before he
went off to the Riviera. He was a dark-haired, slender
young man of about twenty-two, and he laughed self-
consciously as he spoke.

"So what I found," he said, "was that my brother
was killed in the first days of the war, and that everybody in the village was enlisting. They were all joining the same regiment, the Hundred and Fourth. So I
could do nothing but go along."

Marco watched as Marcel took a deep breath and
shrugged. The boy was trying to be casual about the
whole thing, but Marco could see he had been affected
by it. His eyes were fixed on the floor as he went on.
He started telling them all the details, then he seemed
to want to finish it off fast.

"It was just . . . year after year living in trenches. A lot of the men lost fingers and toes from frostbite or died from sickness. Or went crazy. Then we had the big battle of Le Marne. Three days of slaughter. Arms and legs scattered all over. Everybody was half-deaf from the constant bombardments." He tried to smile, but his mouth quivered. "Anyhow, we won the battle. Except . . ." He shrugged again. "I am the only survivor."

Nobody wanted to break the long silence that followed. Bernard Cousseau, the leader of the troupe, finally rose and gave Marcel a pat on the shoulder as he moved past. "I have something that will help you forget," he said. "Come over to my wagon. You too, Marco."

Marco and Marcel followed him out, and Marco glanced at a small wagon parked off by itself as he went up the steps of Bernard's. "Is my mother over there?"

"Yes," Bernard said, "but this will only take a few minutes."

Bernard's wagon looked like a cluttered warehouse of jewelry, clothing, auto parts, silver and gold vases, statuettes and knickknacks, and an assortment of oil paintings. It was hard to find any place to sit. When they were settled, Bernard contemplated his cigar stub for a minute and then held a lighted match under it.

"Marco," he said, "the police were here looking for you a couple of weeks ago. They had a very nice picture of you. I presume that's why you were wearing handcuffs tonight."

"Yes," Marco said. "They decided I was so handsome, they wanted to bring me back to Paris to lift the morale of the ladies."

Marco was glad to see the smile come to Marcel's face, but Bernard was not amused.

"Your escape means they will be coming around here any minute looking for you again. So I think you would be wise to get out of Paris for a while."

Marco nodded. "I may need some money."

"That's what I want to talk to you about. I know where there is a great deal of money. Enough to pay your way anywhere you want to go, and enough to make you forget about Le Marne, Marcel."

"Where is it?"

"In the Swiss embassy. And now that the war is over, I suspect the money will not be there much longer. You see, some of our rich French politicians did not have as much faith in the Allied armies as they might have had. They were particularly worried a few months ago when the Germans were lobbing those big shells into Paris. A great many of them converted their fortunes into Swiss francs and left them in the care of the Swiss ambassador. And to accommodate them, the gentlemen installed a very large safe in one of the upstairs rooms of the embassy. But now that the war is over and Paris is safe, I am sure many of those gentlemen will be making withdrawals very shortly. Thus, the quicker we act, the better."

"Aren't embassies usually guarded by soldiers?" Marco asked.

"Yes, they are. However, the Swiss ambassador is having a very large reception tonight; a gala party to celebrate the Allied victory. So I think you two might join the festivities, and perhaps relieve the ambassador of the heavy responsibility he has in taking care of all that cash."

"Do you know which room has the safe?"

Bernard handed him a small sheet of paper with the layout of the second floor roughly sketched on it. The room with the safe was marked with a red X.

"You and Marcel are both about the same size. I think it might be best if you wear the uniform, Marco. For a corporal to be at such a party might require some fast talking. I'm sure you can handle that, Marco. And Marcel is the best safecracker in Paris."

"I will be happy to wear civilian clothes again," Marcel said with a smile. He quickly rose, unbuttoning his jacket.

"And while you're seeing your mother," Bernard said, "I'll get that dinner jacket cleaned up for Marcel."

Marco's mother was blind in one eye, and she

didn't look well; but she was happy to see him, and a little surprised by the uniform and medals.

"It's for an act we're going to do," he told her after they had embraced.

"You mean you're going to stay with us? What kind of an act?"

"A wonderful act, Mama. One that will make enough money for me to take you back to Spain. Would you like to go back to Spain? I would like to see Sacramonte again."

She reached over and touched his hair. "You are still very handsome, Marco. You look good in the uniform. You would make a fine soldier."

Marco smiled. "I am the son of a great beauty, Mama. I could not help but be handsome."

"You are the son of a gypsy, with a quick silver tongue." She laughed and rumpled his hair.

Marco heard the door jerk open behind him and looked back. It was Bernard.

"Your friends are here, Marco. You'd better hurry."

"All right. Mama," he said, rising. "Think of Spain. Very soon we will go." He kissed her again.

"I will think only of you, my son."

Marcel was waiting in the shadows outside.

"Hugo took care of them for a couple of minutes," Bernard said, "He acted suspicious, like he was scared to death they were going to search his wagon. So now they're searching his wagon, and you'd better go."

Marco hesitated. "Bernard, if I don't come back, promise me you will take care of Mama."

"I promise. But I expect to see both of you before morning."

The Swiss embassy was bright with floodlights, and there was a line of cars bringing guests stretched off for half a block. About half the people stepping out of the cars were military; mostly generals, colonels, and majors. The others appeared to be diplomats and politicians, their wives dressed in diamonds and furs.

Marco smiled as they stood outside the fence and

watched for awhile. If they didn't have a bigger plum in mind, he could walk out of such a party with a million francs' worth of jewelry. It looked as though every woman in Paris had opened her strongbox for the evening.

"Oh-oh," Marco said, peering past the crowd to the front door. "It looks as if this little gathering is more exclusive than Bernard figured. They're all handing over invitations."

Marcel smiled. "Be back in a minute," he said, and moved through the gate, mingling with the people walking toward the door. Marco saw him jostle a fat colonel with a beautiful brunette on his arm. Marcel turned quickly, bowing, offering his apologies to the man, and then he was coming back, smiling.

"We are so sorry, monsieur," he said with a bow to Marco, "No doubt your invitation was misdirected in the mails. The war, you know. The ambassador was most distressed, and has asked me to deliver this personally. He extends his deepest regrets."

Marco laughed and they moved through the gates, following the other guests. When they reached the door, the fat colonel was standing to the side, searching his pockets.

"Is there some problem, mademoiselle?" Marco asked the girl as he handed the invitation to the guard.

The girl looked irritated. "The colonel has lost his invitation."

"*Sacre bleu!*" Marco exclaimed and looked sharply at the guard. "One of France's greatest war heroes, and you have dared to deny him admission for the mere lack of an invitation!" He turned back to the colonel and came stiffly to attention. "I am embarrassed for both France and Switzerland, *mon colonel!* Please take my invitation!"

The colonel blinked, and the guard's face suddenly turned red. He saluted the colonel quickly.

"My most profound apologies, colonel. Please pass."

Marco gave the guard an indignant look and then returned the young lady's warm smile as he and Marcel followed the couple in. *What a pleasant party it might be if they had time,* Marco thought.

The festivities seemed to be spread through a half dozen huge, high-ceilinged rooms, all of them crowded with people. An orchestra was playing syrupy dance music, but few people could find room to dance. They were talking, laughing, and moving around with glasses of champagne in their hands. Marco took two drinks from the tray of a passing waiter, and he and Marcel moved to the side to look things over.

Two grand staircases circled up out of the central room, and people seemed to be moving up and down freely. That made things a little easier. From Bernard's sketch, it appeared that the right-hand staircase would be the best. Then they would have to circle around farther to the right to reach the room with the safe.

"Shall we mingle?" Marco suggested.

"Good idea. Let's do it upstairs."

"Splendid."

They made their way casually through the crowd, smiling, bowing to the ladies as they squeezed through. At the stairway they moved up slowly, appearing to be engrossed in a weighty conversation.

At the top, ladies seemed to be going one way and gentlemen the other. Unfortunately, the ladies' direction was to the right. But they moved that way nevertheless, continuing their conversation, apparently oblivious to their surroundings.

"But of course the artillery broke down, causing the most serious problems," Marco said. "If it had not been for that, we could have brought the tanks in much earlier, and the *Boches* would never have stopped us."

"I agree," Marcel answered, frowning thoughtfully. "But the unit was hopelessly outnumbered from the start. Now, if we had . . ."

They were beyond anybody's hearing now, and after a quick backward glance, they both moved to the door. It was locked, but with Marco shielding him, Marcel inserted a pick. The bolt clicked open in half a minute. They moved quickly inside.

It was a salon of some kind. Delicate needlepoint

chairs and loveseats were ranged around the room. One end had a large fireplace and the other had a tapestry covering half the wall. The two men moved directly to the tapestry. Behind it was a heavy safe, the kind more often seen in banks than in residences.

"What do you think?" Marco asked.

Marcel rubbed his fingers together and looked it over. "I think I can handle it."

"Okay. I'll watch outside."

Marcel was already at work as Marco slipped back through the door. Outside, the corridor was empty. Marco lighted a cigarette, moving casually back to the staircase. There he gazed down at the crowd, searching carefully for anybody who had the appearance of a security guard. Such a man would be doing the same thing he was doing—studying the crowd.

Several moments passed before he realized somebody was staring at him. But it was not a security guard. It was a French colonel standing only three feet away, his wife clinging to his arm, both of them smiling.

"I've been in the service many years, son," the man said, "but I've never earned one of those."

Marco stared back, wondering what the hell the man was talking about. Then he realized it was one of Marcel's medals. He gave the man a cool look, not wanting to encourage conversation. "It is nothing."

"You're very modest, corporal. Which company?"

"The Hundred and Fourth Regiment."

"Ah, yes, the Hundred and Fourth. Le Marne."

"That's right."

"Good regiment. Unfortunately, all my memories of the war are from behind my desk."

"Mine are long nights in trenches with arms and legs being blown off my friends and comrades. And I guess it's hard to earn a medal sitting on your ass behind a desk, colonel." Marco turned sharply and bowed to the woman. "My apologies, madame."

The colonel's face looked as though blood were going to spout from the pores. He turned abruptly and escorted his wife away.

When Marco looked down at the crowd again, he smiled faintly, but then the smile froze, and under his breath he cursed the colonel for taking his time.

Pushing their way through the crowd and coming toward the stairs were two seedy-looking men, obviously from the Sûreté. They must have come in the door about the same time the colonel stopped to admire Marco's medals. Marco quickly turned away as the men glanced up. Then he was running for the room.

Inside, Marcel was still behind the hanging tapestry. Marco locked the door and hurried across. "Have you got it?"

"It's a tough one, Marco."

"Then forget it. There's a couple of detectives on their way up."

"I'll have it in a minute."

"No, we gotta get out of here, Marcel. Fast!"

"Wait a minute—I've got it!" There was a muffled clank and Marcel turned the lever, pulling the heavy door open.

Marco stepped back. Then he heard the doorknob rattle on the other side of the room. *Christ!* he thought. *If we'd only started two minutes earlier!* But it was too late now. He grabbed Marcel's arm. "Come on, we've gotta go out the window!"

There were raised voices in the corridor, and then a crash sent the door flying open.

"Don't move!" the man shouted.

Marco froze, staring at the man and the short-barreled pistol he was holding with both hands. Marco had no intention of moving. Then he gaped in disbelief as Marcel suddenly turned and crouched, a gun exploding again and again in his hand.

Marco had no idea that Marcel was carrying a gun. He was even more shocked to see him firing it. For an instant he was paralyzed, seeing the policeman go down; and then Marcel's face seemed to explode with blood and his head slammed back against the wall. And then Marco was across the room and crashing through a window, hardly conscious of running or choosing the spot where he dove. He felt a sharp pain along the length of his forearm, and then he got a second shock as his head crashed into a steel railing.

He had expected to be flying through the air, groping at nothing and then slamming to the ground. But his flight was no more than five feet—ended by the railing of the balcony. He scrambled quickly to his hands and knees, glancing through the shattered window. Then he vaulted over the railing, holding onto it for an instant to break his momentum. Then he let go, dropping straight down.

Some kind of thorny bushes broke his fall. He rolled quickly to the side and moved into the darker shadows. Then he looked up. He could hear angry voices and the rattle of the broken window being opened. His arm was bloody, but he couldn't worry about that. The man on the balcony would be shouting at the guards any minute now.

His safest escape route would be through the crowd by the front door, Marco decided. Nobody would dare shoot into that many people. He moved along through the high bushes. Then he bolted out across the lawn, angling for the crowd near the gate.

"Halt! Stop or I'll shoot!"

The command came from the balcony behind him, but Marco knew he was safe. People were staring at him, moving to the side as he raced along the walk and through the gate.

"Guards! Stop that man!" the policeman shouted.

Once he was half a block down the street, Marco ducked behind a tree and caught his breath for a minute, watching the traffic go by. His arm was bleeding badly, and he knew he should get a tourniquet on it.

There was a truck coming, moving slowly, and he stared as it passed by. The back was open—eight or ten men sitting inside. Behind him, police whistles were blowing. He made a quick decision, dashing into the street, chasing after the truck.

The men inside laughed as he drew closer. "Give him a hand!" somebody yelled.

Hands reached out just as Marco decided to give

it up. Then he felt his feet hoisted off the ground, and he was suddenly being dragged inside.

"The bastard's bleeding all over the place," somebody said. "He's a goddamned soldier!"

Marco lay still, gasping heavily for breath.

"Roll him over."

"Hey, what happened, buddy?"

Marco rolled over by himself and gazed up at the puzzled faces. "The goddamned Germans," he said. "They're still after me."

A couple of the men laughed, and Marco pulled himself to a sitting position, squeezing the upper part of his arm.

"Look at the medals," somebody said, "He's a bloody hero."

Marco smiled and glanced around. They were a dilapidated-looking lot, most of them unshaven and shabbily dressed. Deeper in the truck there was another man who didn't fit at all. He was wearing tails and a top hat, staring off into space. Marco wondered if he'd jumped into a police van and they were all being hauled off to jail. "Where are you headed?" he asked.

One of the men smiled and pushed his hat back. "First stop is Marseilles. Second stop, I guess, will be Oran, Algeria."

"In *Africa?*"

"That's right. And the end of the line is Morocco."

"You mean you're—?"

"Legionnaires, friend. Join the Legion and see the world. No questions asked."

Marco laughed. Then he looked out at the dark streets of Paris as the truck shifted gears and began to pick up speed.

The French Foreign Legion? He had always figured that a person had to be crazy to join something like that. On the other hand, considering what had just happened, there might be some advantages. Very likely he would be charged with murder—or at least as an accessory to murder. With a policeman dead, there would be a good many angry people looking for him. And even the French police could not arrest a man in the Legion.

"Africa, huh?" he said and smiled. "I've never been to Africa."

IV

Major Foster rested his elbows on the portside railing of the ancient freighter and gazed absently out at the choppy waters of the Mediterranean. An almost full moon had risen shortly after sunset, and its reflection now sparkled and shivered across the surface like a great spotlight following their steady southward progress.

Foster had remained in his stateroom through the day. Their departure from Marseilles had been delayed for three hours while Francois Marneau and his two assistants uncrated and checked over all the equipment and supplies they had shipped down from Paris. They had not pulled out of the harbor until after nine, which meant that it would be after midnight the following day before they reached Oran.

It didn't matter too much one way or the other, but watching Marneau order the sailors and dockworkers around and talk to the ship's captain as if he were a mere seaman, gave Foster an idea of how things were likely to be in the coming months. He wasn't worried about it. If trouble came and there was a crisis, he wouldn't hesitate to clap Marneau in irons and lock him up somewhere. But he would have preferred going out on the desert with somebody who had more sense.

He had spent the day in his stateroom checking over the lists of weapons and equipment they would be taking along to Erfoud, and then going over the roster of personnel. Of the hundred ninety-two men, more than half would be new recruits. There would

41

have to be some hard training in Bousaada before
they headed for the excavation.

Typically, almost half of the recruits appeared to
be Germans. From the list of names, the others came
from all parts of Europe, including even a Russian. But
most of the names were probably aliases, and with the
Legion asking no questions, there was no information
aside from age, height, and weight. They were likely to
be deserters, murderers, thieves, jilted lovers, and a
few deluded souls who had joined hoping to find romance and adventure. Within a week or two, most of
them would regret their decision. They would be looking at the guards and the gates and the desert outside,
assessing their corporals and sergeants and officers,
and wondering if there was a chance in a million to
escape if they deserted. Most of them would see that
they had no choice but to become soldiers. They
would endure the miseries and survive. The others
would get sick and die, or go crazy, or make a suicidal
attempt to slip away and escape across the desert.

Foster's spirits had risen a little once they left
France. The two days in Paris, with all the celebration
and self-congratulating, had depressed him even more
than living in the trenches and fighting an ineptly run
war. It was as if for four years he had been surrounded
by fools, and the more foolish and asinine they were,
the more proud and pleased they were over the disas-
trous results.

Now at least he was on his own, with only one
fool to contend with; and once they reached the desert he would be totally in command. He smiled ruefully, correcting that a little. He would be totally in
command of the expedition and the legionnaires, but
El Krim was likely to have a different idea about who
was in command of the desert.

Foster glimpsed Sergeant Triand step out on the
deck from a passageway, but he didn't move or turn.

"Cigarette, major?"

"Yes. Thanks."

The sergeant lighted both of them with a cupped
match. "I can smell Africa already," he said as he
leaned on the railing.

Foster smiled. The breeze from the southwest had a slight warmth to it, but he could detect no distinctive odor. Sergeant Triand was fifty-two years old and had spent thirty years in Africa. Maybe he had a better idea of its smell.

"Have you taken a look at the recruits?"

"A few, while they were boarding, sir. One of them was wearing a top hat."

Foster smiled again. That would be a man who was probably regretting his decision already. Men like that were generally given a military funeral about three weeks after they got to Africa—which was a waste of a coffin and a flag.

"Have you checked their quarters?"

"No, sir."

Foster didn't comment or tell him to do so. He knew the sergeant would take a look as quickly as he left.

The ship was an old Italian freighter that had probably been confiscated during the war and converted into a short-distance troop carrier. By the clunking sound of its engines and the way it creaked and shuddered, there weren't many trips left in it.

"Have you met the other passengers, sir?"

"You mean there are others besides us and our esteemed scientists?"

"Several others. And a young lady."

Foster glanced at him, but the sergeant's face was expressionless. "Why do you mention the young lady?"

"No reason, sir. She seems to be French, and she appears to be traveling alone."

"So?"

"She's rather . . . interesting-looking, sir."

Foster didn't know how to interpret that. The only interest Triand had ever shown for any women was when he bolted for the Arab brothels whenever they came into a good-sized town. "What do you mean, 'interesting-looking'?"

"Well, I don't know, sir. Classy, I guess you might say. Sort of aloof. Friendly, but aloof. I'm sure you'll see her at dinner. Very attractive, I think."

Foster still wasn't sure what Triand was saying.
An expensive prostitute could be attractive, friendly,
and aloof, and would probably look like a princess to
Triand. And that was likely to be the profession of a
young French lady traveling to Oran by herself.

"I think I'll have a look at the men's quarters,
sir."

Foster nodded. After the sergeant was gone, he
flicked his cigarette into the wind and reflected on what
a small part women had played in his life. Actually,
he wasn't too much different from Sergeant Triand,
and as often as not he went along with him to the
brothels. But he had no regrets about it. He had seen
too many Legion officers settle down in Oran, or Algiers, or Marrakesh and become domesticated. That's
when they started calculating how much pension they
could get, and how they could keep as far away from
marauding Arabs as possible.

Or else they became colonels and generals with
offices in Paris, and they and their wives hated people
like Foster. It was interesting how women always
wanted a nest and somebody to protect it, and then
they hated anybody who was a good soldier and did
his duty giving them that protection. Wars and vio-
lence were necessary things to keep peace in the world
or bring civilization to the savages; but in women's
eyes, anybody who was efficient at it was a beast and a
barbarian. So be it, Foster reflected. At least with prostitutes, a man didn't have to listen to their opinions.

He finally moved away from the railing to the
door leading into the dining room. One of the crew
members had come around twenty minutes earlier an-
nouncing that dinner was being served, but Foster had
not been particularly hungry.

The dining room was divided into two parts, half
of it a lounge area with a piano and upholstered chairs
and a small bar. Five or six people were already eating, and Foster moved across to where Marneau and
his assistants were talking casually to several other
people at the bar.

"Ah, Major Foster," Marneau smiled. "We were

about to dine. Won't you join us? And may I present Madame and Monsieur Durand, and Madame Picard. And of course you know my two assistants, Monsieur Ranier and Monsieur Mollard."

The Durands were an elderly couple, the type of people one always saw at expensive, but not quite luxurious hotels. Foster guessed Monsieur Durand was a retired merchant; the kind of man who was neither offensive nor interesting.

Foster nodded and then found himself staring at the woman Marneau had introduced as Madame Picard. There was no doubt about her being the young lady Triand said was "attractive." The description was a considerable understatement.

In Paris Foster had seen any number of women who might have been described as striking or beautiful —from those on the Champs-Élysées to the ones who appeared at all the generals' cocktail parties. But if Madame Picard had ever attended such gatherings, he had no doubt that all the other women were ignored.

She was dressed simply, and had no discernible makeup, but she was stunning—a rare combination of classic and sensual beauty that Foster had never seen in a woman before. He could easily imagine every artist in Paris clamoring to paint her portrait. And no doubt every man to whom she was introduced stared speechlessly at her—just as he was doing.

"How do you do, major," she said without smiling.

"Very well, thank you, madame," Foster said.

There was a distant, almost sad look in her eyes as she turned and placed her empty glass on the bar.

"Isn't it rather unusual for an American to be in the French Foreign Legion, Major Foster?" Durand asked.

"I don't think so, monsieur. Isn't that what the word 'foreign' means?"

"Are you a hero, major?" his wife asked. "Someone important?"

"There are no heroes in wars, madame—only survivors."

They were moving to the tables, and Foster found himself next to the younger woman. He drew out a chair for her and took the next one for himself.

"I just adore Morocco," Madame Durand was saying. "Don't you, Madame Picard?"

She seemed to consider the question for a minute. Then she smiled politely. "No, madame, I'm afraid I don't."

"Oh. Then you've been there before?"

"No, I haven't."

It was an odd conversation, and Foster couldn't help smiling to himself. The young lady seemed to know her mind, whether her answers made any sense or not.

"You have to give Morocco a chance," Durand said enthusiastically. "It's—well, another world. Exotic people, strange customs. I think you will find it very interesting." He smiled at the three archaeologists. "Have you gentlemen been to Morocco?"

"Many times," Marneau answered.

"Before the war, of course," Mollard added. "We're going to Morocco for the Louvre."

Madame Durand gave the man a stern look. "What the Louvre needs is some heat in the bathrooms. I think it's scandalous to have such poor accommodations in such a famous museum!"

Foster suddenly found himself liking the older woman. She had a lot more sense than Francois Marneau.

"I toast you gentlemen," Durand said and lifted his wineglass. "To the Louvre!"

Foster noticed that Madame Picard gave the man a cold glance and did not touch her glass.

"What in the world are you going to do for the Louvre in Morocco?" Madame Durand asked.

"We are conducting an excavation, madame. We intend to bring a part of that great culture back to France."

The woman looked puzzled and glanced at Foster.

"It is called graverobbing, madame," he said. "In many parts of the world, people are hanged for it."

"Is that a soldier's view of art?" Marneau said sharply.

"It is if you can find the tomb."

"I can find it, major."

"Perhaps," Foster said. "And after you empty it, the Arabs will fill it with the bodies of my legionnaires."

Marneau's face reddened and he glared at Foster. "You are an officer, Major Foster, but you speak like a foot soldier."

"I speak *for* the foot soldier, Monsieur Marneau. That is why I am an officer. I see no art in sending men to their deaths."

"Perhaps we have a different perspective, major. I speak for the people of France, and in the interests of permanent beauty."

"And I speak for men's lives."

"Gentlemen!" Durand broke in. "Perhaps we should change——"

Marneau ignored him. "Do you realize, major, how easy it is to make life? An Arab peasant girl can do it. But to make beauty that enriches life—that is difficult."

"Actually," Madame Durand said, "it's the Arab women I feel sorry for. The poor things have to do all the work for the men. And then the men won't even let the women eat with them."

"Don't waste your pity," Foster said. "They're not worth it."

"On the contrary, Major Foster, I think anybody is worth our pity."

Foster gazed at his plate, then gave her a cool smile. "Madame, when a legionnaire is taken prisoner by a desert tribe, he is given to the women. You see, there are not many ways for Arab women to entertain themselves in the desert. No social teas, no country-club dances, no shipboard dinners."

Marneau was glaring at him again. "Major Foster, I hardly think this is the place——"

"The Arab women kill the prisoners," Foster went on quietly, "but they take their time about it. First they

strip the men naked. Then they tie their arms and legs
to stakes in the ground, and then they use knives. The
Arab women are very skilled with knives. They know
thousands of ways to cut a man without killing him.
Sometimes it takes three days for a man to die."

The little speech was not so much for Madame
Durand's benefit as it was for Marneau. But they were
all staring at him now, aghast.

"I am sorry, ladies and gentlemen," Foster said
coolly, "but that is Morocco, and those are some of the
exotic people and their strange customs."

Madame Picard suddenly placed her napkin on
the table and rose. "Excuse me, please," she said
calmly.

Foster quickly helped her with the chair, noticing
that she had touched none of her dinner. She gave him
a faint smile and quietly went out the door leading to
the deck.

"What time are we expected to arrive in Oran tomorrow?" Durand asked, directing the question to nobody in particular.

Marco had some doubts about having enlisted in
the Legion. Once the truck had reached Marseilles, he
would have gladly slipped away, and probably would
have had no trouble finding a small packet or fishing
boat that might have taken him to Italy or Spain. But
the truck drove directly into an ancient fort several
miles from the city, and then guards were on all sides
of them, apparently anticipating some disenchantment
from the recruits. From the truck they were herded
into barracks, where roll call was taken, and then a
sergeant-major glared suspiciously at Marco and de-
manded to know who he was and why his arm was all
bloody and how he got into the truck. By then the
officer of the guards had been summoned, and there
seemed to be some discussion about whether he should
be shot or placed permanently in the guardhouse.

So Marco told the truth. Since he was six years
old, he explained, he had always wanted to be a legionnaire and kill Arabs in Africa. It was only because he had some difficulty getting back from Le

Marne that he had missed the recruiting officer in Paris, but in the hope that he might enlist in Marseilles, he had jumped on the truck just as it departed from the recruiting office. As to the wound, a frustrated German officer had inflicted it three days after the armistice had been signed. The lieutenant had stared at him for a full minute and then ordered the sergeant-major to get an enlistment form—which Marco promptly signed.

At four o'clock the next morning they were marched to the docks and as they filed into the hold of the old Italian freighter, each man was handed a blanket. Five hours later, the ship had limped and vibrated out of the harbor, and Marco was no longer a free man.

Along with the other recruits, he slept most of the day. At noon each man was given a bowl of soup and a piece of bread, and at seven o'clock the same rations were issued, along with a quarter-liter of wine. Marco ate the meal in a dark corner of the hold and then lit a cigarette and had a look around.

Recruits were permitted only on the aft section of the main deck. To go above that a man had to be able to prove he was a human being, which meant that he had to be a civilian or an officer. The guard at the bottom of the steel stairway advised Marco of this and told him to get his ass moving. Marco thanked him and moved on.

On the deck it was too dark to make out any faces. Lighted cigarettes were visible here and there, and about half of the men sitting around appeared to be veterans. Marco threaded his way slowly through the crowd, and then spotted the shape of a top hat off to the side.

They were all there, the men who had pulled him into the truck in Paris. He found a place to sit where he could rest his back against the side.

"Only four years and three hundred and sixty-four days to go," he said.

They chuckled, but they all seemed preoccupied. Some were staring off at nothing, the others looking at the upper decks.

"That's some fur coat you've got there," Marco said to the man squatted across from him. He was a huge Russian who hadn't spoken a word on the trip down from Paris. Somebody had said his name was Ivan. "You kill a bear up in Siberia, Ivan?"

The man stared at him through half-closed eyes.

"I joined the Legion because I missed the war," the kid next to Marco said as if somebody had asked. He looked as if he was about eighteen and straight out of an English prep school. "I actually told my parents I was going on holiday to see the battlefields." He laughed nervously and straightened a pair of glasses with a crack across one lens. "They're going to be furious when they find out. My name's Fred, by the way." He stuck out a hand and Marco shook it.

"The last time Mummy and Daddy took me on a boat trip, we went to Italy," he said. "First-class, of course. I must say, it's the only way to travel."

Fred didn't seem to be generating much enthusiasm, but he kept trying. He smiled at Ivan.

"You look like a man who's traveled first-class."

Ivan still had his brooding stare and Marco smiled. "Ivan travels first-class all the time, Fred."

"How do you know?" Top-hat asked.

"He told me."

"I haven't heard him say a word in two days."

"Well, Ivan and I have an understanding. Isn't that right, Ivan?"

Either Ivan didn't understand French, or he was deaf and dumb. His eyes moved slowly to Top-hat and back to Marco.

"Were you with the Hundred and Fourth?" Fred suddenly asked.

Marco nodded, thinking about Marcel.

"Then you were at Le Marne. Is that where you got those medals?"

He had forgotten about the medals. He looked down and pulled them off one by one, staring at them in his hand. Then he silently dropped them over the rail.

"I'm sorry," Fred said.

"It's okay," Marco answered. As he spoke a big

floodlight suddenly came on, illuminating most of the deck. Apparently somebody wanted to take a look at them.

It was a grizzled old sergeant with a face like the hide of a turtle. The guard quickly unlatched the chain across the stairway and the sergeant came down wearing the expression of a man surveying a cesspool. A couple of the veterans said something to him, and he grunted a response.

"How are things with the major?" a man sitting farther along the rail yelled out. Marco couldn't see the man, but from the sneering tone it didn't sound as though he was a friend of the sergeant's.

There was no change in the sergeant's expression, but he shifted course slightly, moving toward the questioner. Then he stopped and gazed impassively at the man.

"I thought Foster would have gotten himself a new sergeant by now," the questioner said. "Aren't you getting a little old to be holding his hand, Triand?" The man made a kissing sound, and a few of the veteran legionnaires laughed.

The movement came so fast that for a minute Marco wasn't sure what was happening. The sergeant suddenly reached forward and straightened, yanking the legionnaire to his feet. As quickly as the man was up, the sergeant cracked him hard across the jaw, and he was down again.

Suddenly a dozen veterans were on their feet, moving cautiously away from the two men. Marco saw the flash of a knife as the legionnaire crouched and came at the sergeant. Then the man was staggered by another blow, and the knife flew off into the crowd. For a moment, the two of them were locked together, half-wrestling as they pounded each other. Then the legionnaire's body suddenly rose horizontally above the crowd. The sergeant had the man by the belt and the throat, and with two long steps he heaved him over the railing.

Marco stared, and for half a minute there wasn't a sound anywhere on the deck. Then somebody laughed and turned away. As if he had done nothing more than stop to chat or light a cigarette, the sergeant moved on, looking the men over, finally circling back to the stairs. When he reached the upper deck, the floodlight went off.

Marco eased down again and glanced at Fred. The kid was frowning, as if he wasn't too sure what to make of what he had seen.

"Maybe we don't have four years and three hundred and sixty-four more days," Top-hat said glumly.

It was hard to tell what age Top-hat was. There were no wrinkles or creases in his face, but there were enough frayed edges to suggest he was past thirty. He was either a young man who had done a lot of drinking, or an older man who had taken care of himself.

"You know, gentlemen," Marco said, looking at the upper deck, "I'm inclined to think there must have been some kind of mix-up in our accommodations."

An elegant-looking couple was standing by the railing above them. They were dressed as if they had just come from a fancy cocktail party, both of them holding cognac snifters as they gazed out at the water.

"Top-hat," Marco said as they all looked, "Did you book with Cook's Tours?"

Top-hat frowned at him, then smiled. "Oh, indeed. I wouldn't think of letting anybody else handle the arrangements."

"Well, as I recall, the deluxe Moroccan tour includes cocktails and aperitifs, doesn't it?"

Top-hat nodded. "I certainly wouldn't have come if it didn't. You got any ideas?"

Marco got to his feet and surveyed the situation. "A gypsy always has ideas, Top-hat."

The staircase with the guard was on the other side of the deck, and the man wouldn't be able to see if Marco moved forward along the railing. Once he was out of sight, it didn't look as if it would be too hard to climb the steel girders going up the side of the ship. He took a last look at the guard and moved casually away, his hands stuck in his rear pockets.

The dampness on the slick paint made things a little harder than he had expected. But once he had inched his way up the girder and grasped a post on the upper deck, he swung a leg up and slid easily beneath the lower railing. As he rose to his feet, he heard some cheering from the lower deck.

Music was coming from somewhere up ahead. Marco moved along the deck and under the bridge wing until he came to a lighted window. There he could see a violinist and a man sitting at a piano. It was a lounge of some sort, with two or three couples sitting at tables. On the far side of the room, a dozen or so people, including a Legion officer, were eating dinner.

Marco smiled and stepped through the open door, moving past the piano and over to an elderly couple who had a bottle of cognac on their table.

"Good evening, madame, monsieur. Did you enjoy your dinners?"

The man blinked at him, apparently puzzled by the appearance of an army corporal. "Well—yes, thank you," he said.

"Splendid." Marco lifted the bottle of cognac and studied the label. "Ahhh, a good year. May I have some?"

The woman gave him an amused smile. "Why, yes —of course."

"You are very kind, madame." Marco leaned forward with his hand on the clasp of the woman's pearl necklace and kissed her. Then he smiled and strode out with the bottle.

"Mes amis!" he shouted when he returned to the rear of the deck. He held the bottle up and then gave it a long, easy toss into the outstretched hands. When he turned back, he stopped short.

He hadn't noticed the young lady at all when he moved along the deck and stepped into the lounge. But she must have seen everything. She was standing at the railing just opposite the door, partially hidden by the shadow of a lifeboat. Now she was gazing coolly at him, not particularly amused.

She was a beautiful woman—the kind Marco had sometimes seen on the arms of millionaires in Cannes and Monaco. But she looked more sophisticated than most of those. Marco smiled and moved to the rail next to her. "Have I kept you waiting, my dear?"

She turned and looked out at the water.

Marco glanced behind him, then crossed to the open door. "Pssst! Artistes!" he said to the musicians. "Play some gypsy music—romantic music!"

The violinist smiled and quickly responded, moving to the door as he played.

"Madame?" Marco said, touching the woman's elbow. "May I have this dance?"

She smiled slightly, but she didn't move away from the rail. "I'm sorry, I don't dance with strangers."

"I am no stranger, madame. I am Marco. None of the people who know me think I am a stranger." He took her hand, smiling, holding it high as he drew her away from the rail. "And what is your name?"

"All of the people who know me know my name," she countered. She danced, but kept her distance.

"Of course. You are Venus de Milo. Or is it Helen of Troy? Didn't we have a drink together in Troy?"

She smiled. "It is Madame Picard."

"Madame Picard," Marco repeated. "That is not a name, it is a title."

"Simone."

Marco laughed and whirled her around with a dramatic flair, moving to the rear of the deck in full view of the legionnaires. They were cheering and whistling now, some of them shouting for him to bring her down.

Marco only caught a glimpse of the guard as he disappeared on the other side of the deck, but he knew what it meant.

"Is it midnight yet?" he asked, drawing the girl closer.

"I don't think so, why?"

"Because I am going to turn into a pumpkin in a very few minutes." He fished the pearl necklace from his pocket and pressed it into her hand. "A gift from my gypsy mother," he whispered. *"Au revoir."*

"Hold it, soldier!"

Marco had almost reached the top of the staircase

when the angry command cracked the air. He hesitated, but then thought better of continuing down the
stairs. He came to attention and gave a sharp salute.
"At your service, my colonel!"

Major Foster had just left the table to go back to
his stateroom when he saw the guard talking excitedly
to Triand.

"What's the trouble, sergeant?" he asked.

"It's one of the recruits, sir. He's up on the passenger deck, dancing with—with that young lady."

Normally Foster didn't bother with disciplining
recruits. There were plenty of sergeants and corporals
around who knew how to crack heads. But hearing
that the man was dancing with Madame Picard surprised him.

"I'll take care of it, sergeant," he said and strode
out on the deck.

It was Triand who commanded the man to stop.
Foster saw the woman standing on the other side, but
he gave her only a quick glance.

"What are you doing here, mister?" he asked
after the man saluted.

"It was for the men, sir. After the hardships we
have endured, it seemed clear that they needed some
cognac to boost their spirits."

Foster smiled coldly to himself. He had seen
jokers like this before. He had seen them locked in
sweatboxes, and lying out in the sun with their hands
and feet tied at the middle of their backs. What he
had never seen was one of them who turned into a decent soldier.

"Sergeant! Bring a bottle of cognac."

"Yes, sir."

"What's your name, mister?"

"Marco. They call me the gypsy."

Foster looked over the uniform and at the spot
where the medals had been torn away. He was a little
surprised that a man from the army didn't know better. On the other hand, having seen a good deal of the
regular army soldiers, maybe he shouldn't be surprised.

"Well, gypsy, we in the Legion like to make a new man welcome. Make him feel he's among friends. His home away from home."

Marco nodded and Triand was suddenly back with a bottle of cognac and a water tumbler.

"Pour him a drink, sergeant," Foster said. "Do you know anything about the Legion, mister?"

"Not very much."

"Sir."

"Sir," Marco said.

"Give the man his drink, sergeant."

The glass was filled to the top, and Marco glanced from the major to the sergeant as he took it.

"The Legion is the best army in the world. The *world*, mister. Drink it!"

Marco sipped at the glass.

"All of it, mister. Fast!"

It was clear to Marco what was going to happen, and that there was nothing he could do about it. He drained the glass.

"Fill it up, sergeant. Do you know why the Legion is the best army in the world, mister? Because it is the best disciplined. Drink, mister."

Marco downed half of it, then blinked and swallowed the rest.

"And this is your first lesson in discipline. Sergeant, the man's glass is empty."

Triand filled it again and Marco glanced at Simone. She was watching, her face expressionless.

"Eyes front, mister. Drink!"

Marco forced it down, gagging with the last gulps.

"I think the man is still thirsty, sergeant. Give him another."

Marco's eyes lost their focus and his stomach jumped. He took a deep breath and then blinked hazily as he took the glass. He had never been a heavy drinker, and his stomach was reminding him of the fact.

"Major, I think he's had enough."

The comment came from Madame Picard. Foster turned sharply, giving her a hard stare. She was gazing calmly at him, her chin lifted.

Foster turned back, suddenly feeling his face flush

with anger. If the woman had her way, she would probably have him slap the gypsy's hands and ask the man politely not to do it again.

"Drink it!" he ordered.

Marco smiled woozily across at the girl and then lifted the glass. He gagged at the first taste of it. Then he closed his eyes and gulped until the tumbler was empty. When the glass came down, it slipped from his hand and dropped to the deck.

"Discipline, mister," Foster said. "And don't you ever forget it! Dismissed!"

Marco reached for the railing and staggered to the stairs. The guard stepped aside and gave him a push which sent him tumbling down.

Foster watched as the man slowly picked himself up from the lower deck and staggered off. Then he bowed stiffly toward the young woman. "Madame," he said and walked away.

Something puzzled him about the gypsy. He had seen that man somewhere before, but he couldn't place it. At the front? In Paris?

When he returned to his stateroom, Foster stood at the porthole and gazed out at the darkness for several minutes before it finally came to him. It was in Paris—in front of the Swiss embassy.

Foster had not wanted to go to the party, but when he went around to pick up his orders, Colonel Dechamps insisted, telling him that he needed some recreation before he returned to Africa. When he and the colonel were approaching the door, a corporal with some medals was berating the guard for not letting a French colonel into the party without an invitation. Ten minutes later, there was a shooting in one of the upstairs rooms, and a corporal wearing medals had escaped through a window. Marco the gypsy must have been that corporal.

Interesting, Foster thought. *It wasn't the first time that a murderer had joined the French Foreign Legion.* But he had a feeling that a little extra effort was going to be needed to turn this one into a soldier.

V

Traveling west from Oran the first day, the train carrying the legionnaires passed through country that was surprisingly fertile. Date groves and farms and orchards and irrigated fields, all rich with a variety of crops spread out on both sides of them. It was not until the next day when they crossed the border into Morocco and passed through a range of mountains to the south that they came into the desert. Then the dust and sand and the ashes from the engine poured steadily through the cattle cars where the legionnaires were riding.

The recruits had been issued uniforms at the fort in Oran, and now they had the look of soldiers. But most of them slept or sat with their heads curled between their knees to avoid the blowing sand and grit.

Could he have escaped in Oran? Marco wondered now, and wished he had tried. He wasn't likely to get any more chances that good. It had been three o'clock in the morning when the ship docked, and marching through the dark streets there were hundreds of alleys he might have ducked into. With the guards as tired and sleepy as the men, he doubted if they would have noticed him, or chased after him if they did. He might even have gotten back to the harbor and stolen a boat before sunrise. But now, with the desert growing larger and hotter, and only a few isolated Arab settlements sitting out in nowhere, he had grave doubts about anybody's chances of getting back to civilization.

After his run-in with Foster that night, he had vomited most of the cognac over the side of the ship. But enough had stayed with him that he spent the rest of the trip curled up on his blanket in the hold. Top-hat and Fred brought him meals and a cup of wine that helped. And then the corporal was kicking him awake, and half an hour later they were stumbling through the streets of Oran. So he had probably missed his only chance.

Marco had no illusions about what kind of a soldier he would make. He could imagine no better way for a man to waste his life than to spend it sitting around barracks or marching across deserts with hundred-pound packs. Even shooting Arabs seemed a waste of time, because from what he had seen of Algeria and Morocco, the Legion didn't have enough bullets to kill half of them.

Most of the second day on the train he sat with Ivan and Fred and Top-hat—like everybody else keeping his head down to protect it from the heat and the stinging sand and dust. And then he stood at the open door for a while and stared out at the endless miles of empty desert. What seemed amazing was that the Arabs had bothered to claim a country like this in the first place, and that the French had bothered to take it away from them.

Most of the time while he sat in the car or looked out at the desert, he found himself thinking about Simone Picard. He wondered where she had come from and where she was going, and who Monsieur Picard might be. Not that it made any difference. Trapped in the Foreign Legion, he was not likely to see her again, and he was not even sure she was on the train with them. She could have met her husband in Oran, or maybe she had stayed on the ship and gone on to Algiers.

If he had met her a week ago on the Riviera, he wondered if he would have been impressed with the girl. Or was he a poor soldier falling in love on the day he was shipped off to war?

Marco laughed at the idea. He turned his kepi

around so the skirt covered his face and tried to sleep for a while. Then he got restlessly to his feet again and stepped over legionnaires to get back to the door.

He could see nothing ahead but more empty desert stretching out for endless miles. He finally looked up at the top of the car and smiled. At least there was one thing he could get settled—whether or not Simone Picard was still in Oran, or if she was somewhere on the train and going to Bousaada.

Using the open side-boards for a ladder he climbed easily to the top of the cattle car. Then he moved forward, jumping to the car in front of it. A few of the men inside looked up indifferently as he tightroped his way along the narrow boards. After the third jump, he was on the roof of a passenger car, and he took a good grip and then stretched himself far over the side and peered in.

It was a stateroom with a gray-haired man reading a newspaper—his wife starting to pull her dress over her head. The woman suddenly looked over and gaped at him and Marco smiled, pulling himself back up to the roof.

About half the seats of the next car were occupied, a good many of the people sleeping. Marco dangled just below the edge of the window again and scanned the seats and the assortment of heads. Then his heart jumped and he grinned. There was no question about it—seated next to a window near the front of the car was a beautiful head of blonde hair. He swung back up and moved quickly to a position just above the seat and eased himself over, smiling as he worked his head below the top of the window.

"Come to the back of the car!" he shouted when she gave him a startled look. He pointed toward the rear, and she seemed to get the idea. She shook her head in disbelief and finally rose.

She was already there when he swung down to the observation platform. "Are you looking for another drink, Mr. Gypsy?" she asked with a half-smile.

"No," Marco grinned, "I was hoping a fairy princess might come out for a breath of air. How are you?"

She looked more beautiful than ever. Her eyes

were green, Marco noticed, and she had a beautiful mouth.

"I am very well," she said. "And I met your mother on the ship the other night."

"My mother?"

"Yes. It seems that she had misplaced her pearl necklace. Apparently she forgot that she had given it to you. She was very happy to get it back."

"Ahhh, my mother. Yes, she is very forgetful sometimes." Marco grinned, and she gave him a look of mock disapproval.

"Are you really a gypsy?" she asked.

"I am at least half-gypsy. Give me your hand and I will prove it."

"What is the other half?"

"Some say it was a Norwegian fire-eater. Others say it was a German tightrope artist. Personally I have always suspected it was a French juggler named Georges." He took her hand, then looked up sharply. "Why are you going to Bousaada?"

The question seemed to startle her. Then she shrugged. "I am not sure. Perhaps you can find the reason in my palm."

There were a lot more things Marco wanted to ask her. Would she go to Tangier with him if he deserted from the Legion? Would she consider living on the Riviera with a jewel thief? No—for this girl he would give up stealing. He would become a respectable businessman, a farmer, a crooked politician—anything she wanted.

She was leaning against the door of the railroad car, smiling skeptically at him. "Well, what do you see?"

Marco frowned at the hand. "I see a very long life . . . good health . . . a drastic change in your way of living . . . Monsieur Picard—is he ill?"

She gazed calmly at him, not answering.

"I also see travel. Perhaps a long trip with a new acquaintance."

She smiled. "A man in a uniform, perhaps?"

Marco kissed the hand and let it go. "Yes, perhaps with a man in a uniform."

She looked at her hand. "Where did you see that?"

"I didn't see it anywhere. I felt your hand tremble when I kissed it."

He touched her cheek and gently cupped her face in both hands as he kissed her. There was no resistance.

"Now I am certain," he said as he drew back.

Was her smile one of pleasure, or merely amusement? Marco couldn't tell. He grinned and pulled himself up on the railing, then paused before swinging to the roof. He held up a pair of earrings and studied them for a minute. "They are beautiful."

Her mouth came open and she quickly touched an ear. Then she laughed. "Keep them," she said. "For good luck."

Marco smiled and stuffed them in a pocket. Then he swung to the roof and headed back along the wobbling cars. No, he thought, it was not so ridiculous for him to be in love.

It was late afternoon and the train was thirty miles from Bousaada when Major Foster saw the first of El Krim's Arab warriors. At the time he was glancing through reports from General Lyautey, the colonial administrator of Morocco, and he happened to look off at the desert for a minute when he spotted the man. It was a lone camel-mounted sentry standing on a sand dune almost a mile ahead of them. But there was no question about the rich blue color of his djellaba. Foster absently returned the reports to the open briefcase and gazed out the window for another minute, studying the man. The Arab's rifle was slung across his back and he was facing the train, watching it, not moving. The man was at least sixty miles away from home. Foster rose and put on his kepi, moving to the front of the car.

"Sergeant!" he said, and motioned Triand to come with him.

Between the cars he could lean out far enough to see all of them—about two hundred mounted Arabs straddling the tracks a mile and a half ahead.

"El Krim?" Triand asked. He was leaning out behind Foster, hanging onto his hat.

Foster nodded. They were El Krim's men, but it was hard to tell if El Krim was with them. They all looked well armed. A quarter-mile closer, a man was standing beside the tracks holding a crude white flag.

The conductor burst through the door just as Foster stepped back. "Major, there's a bunch of Arabs blocking the tracks ahead. I've told the engineer to go full speed ahead. You'd better tell your men."

Foster brushed past the man and went back inside the car. "Ladies and gentlemen," he announced, "there are some Arabs on the tracks ahead, and we're stopping. I don't want anyone to leave his seat, and if any of you have firearms, do not use them."

Marneau was suddenly on his feet, moving up the aisle. "Stopping? My God, man, are you—?"

Foster turned away and gave the emergency cord a hard pull. "Alert the men, sergeant, and pass out rifles to the veterans. But there is to be no firing unless I give the order."

The train shuddered, the cars swaying and bucking as the brakes suddenly came on.

"But, major—" the conductor protested, following Foster through the door again.

"Shut up and take care of your passengers!"

Foster leaned out between the cars and watched as the wheels screeched and chattered and the train began to slow.

They were passing the first scattering of Arabs now, their rifles resting across saddles and their dark, brooding eyes staring out from covered faces. It was always hard to tell what an Arab had in mind until he decided to do it. Then it would come with a wild charge and blood-curdling screams. The train shuddered once again and finally ground to a stop, the engine panting and hissing impatiently.

With the Arabs silently watching him, Foster stepped down easily and moved a few paces away from the tracks. From the cars at the back he could hear the bolts of rifles being thrown as bullets were shoved into chambers. He hoped the Arabs heard it, too, and thought all two hundred men had rifles. Then he saw the movement: fifteen or twenty camels coming around the front of the engine, walking leisurely toward him. In the center of the group El Krim's orange and green djellaba was in sharp contrast to the varying shades of blue. Foster watched, expressionless as they approached. What did not please him was the number of new rifles El Krim's men seemed to have. Then those in front moved to the sides, giving El Krim an open path.

Was he smiling, or only squinting, assessing the situation? The camel stopped and the dark eyes regarded Foster for a moment before they shifted, studying the train and the armed legionnaires in the last three cars. Then his stick touched the camel's shoulder and the animal quickly crouched. El Krim slid from the saddle and strode forward, clearly smiling now.

"Welcome, Foster," he said and laughed, lifting his arms.

Foster moved forward, meeting him halfway to return the embrace. When he finally stepped back, he smiled.

The Arab chieftain looked no different from four years earlier. He was a powerfully built man with a stiff salt-and-pepper goatee and four or five deep scars on his face.

"I am surprised, Foster," El Krim said. "I did not expect to see you in the desert again."

"A soldier goes where he is sent."

"So it is written. And I see you have brought three cages-full of young men with you. Are they prepared to die for the glory of France?"

"If necessary."

"Of course it is necessary, old friend." El Krim laughed. "For France to have any glory in the desert, it will be necessary for all the young men of France to die."

Foster nodded, wondering if there might not be some truth in that. "I have orders from the premier of France to reopen the excavation at Erfoud."

El Krim gazed coldly at him for a minute. "I see. And from Allah I have orders to stop you, my friend. I marvel at the French audacity in thinking they have the right to divide up other people's property. I marvel even more at their foolishness in sending more troops to try to do it." He glanced at the rear of the train. "You can bring ten thousand trainloads of legionnaires, Foster, and you will still take nothing from our homeland."

El Krim smiled, but it was clearly a warning. And publicly announced, it meant there was little possibility of later negotiations.

"I am sorry, El Krim. I shall do as I have been ordered."

"And I shall do as Allah wills," the Arab said softly.

Foster nodded and turned sharply back to the railroad car.

"Foster!"

Foster stopped, surprised to see the Arab smiling at him.

"I have a present for you, major."

El Krim motioned and a smiling Arab suddenly appeared, carrying a large sack. Ten feet from Foster, the man stopped, flinging the contents out on the sand.

"Deserters," El Krim said with a sneer. "You usually pay for them."

Foster had an idea what was in the sacks, but he was still shocked. The three severed heads had rolled across the sand and come to rest almost at his feet. One of them had stopped face-down with the stripped-away scalp dangling from the back of the skull. The other two had their eyelids cut away and seemed to be staring up at him as if frightened and pleading for help. One of the mouths was stuffed with the man's genitals, while the other's lips and nose and ears had been sliced off and a ludicrous smile painted across the face.

The Arabs were all grinning when Foster looked up—most of them watching the windows of the railroad cars, amused by the horrified reactions from the passengers.

"And now, Foster," El Krim said, "I have an even better present for the premier of France."

Foster took a deep breath and braced himself,

knowing El Krim would have saved the worst for last. He watched as four Arabs came through the crowd dragging two large wicker cages between them. As quickly as the cages were set down, El Krim nodded, and the men whipped off the burlap coverings.

"I believe their names are Henri and Pierre, major," El Krim said. "They were digging for trinkets at Erfoud when we found them."

The two men were still alive, but most of their flesh was in ragged strips. The white bone of ribs and elbows and kneecaps was visible, and masses of flies swarmed around the open wounds. The eyes and tongues of both men had been removed and were in pottery bowls in front of them.

Foster stared at the sickening spectacle for a minute, wondering how the Arabs had kept them alive through the butchery. The man on the left was swinging his head back and forth, groaning unintelligibly. The other was leaning heavily against the side of the cage, opening and closing his tongueless mouth as if trying to work the flies out.

"You've changed, El Krim," Foster said quietly. "Apparently you have become a woman and learned to enjoy watching men suffer."

It was the strongest insult anyone could deliver to a man like El Krim. The Arab chieftain's head lifted and he glared at Foster.

In the silence Foster opened his holster and drew out his pistol, aiming it carefully at the archaeologist's swinging head. He fired quickly; the man's head jerked back and he slumped silently to the side.

There were angry murmurs and the sound of rifle bolts being thrown, but Foster ignored them. He turned the pistol to the second man and quickly fired again, hitting him squarely in the forehead.

With the pistol hanging at his side, he gazed evenly at El Krim for a minute. Then he turned and boarded the train.

"Signal the engineer to go ahead," he told the conductor.

"But the two men—"

"We are leaving! Signal him! Now!" Foster glared at the man until the signal was given.

Inside the car, his passage was blocked by Madame Durand, who stood in the aisle, her face flushed and indignant.

"Good Lord!" she exclaimed, "I have never seen such cold-blooded— It is you who are the barbarian, Major Foster!"

"Excuse me, madame," he said and tried to pass.

The woman was almost hysterical, suddenly pointing at a seat near the front. "Did you know that one of those men is Madame Picard's father? It is you who should be shot, major! You are a murderer!"

Foster looked at Madame Picard. She was sitting stiffly in her seat, her eyes fixed vacantly on some point directly ahead, as if too shocked to move.

"Excuse me, madame," Foster said and squeezed past Madame Durand.

He ignored the stares of Marneau and his two assistants as he strode past. In his seat he placed General Lyautey's reports on his lap again and gazed irritably out the window as he tried to control his anger.

He did not enjoy killing people, and it was unfortunate that one of the men had been Madame Picard's father. But he had not asked the man to come to Morocco to rob graves, nor had he asked Madame Picard or any of these people to come and observe the brutality of life in the Moroccan desert. As to Marneau and his assistants, maybe it would give them a small idea of the price people paid to enrich the treasures of the Louvre.

VI

The recruits were a ragged, flabby-looking bunch. No more than ten or twelve of them appeared to be fit, or to have any idea what was in store for them. Foster moved slowly along the first row, glancing at each man. Then he doubled back looking at those in the rear. As usual, there were a good many Germans, along with a mixture of Serbs and Croats and Slovaks. The temperature was no more than a hundred degrees, but they were all sweating like pigs, the accumulation of fat and flab and wine and easy living being baked out of them.

"What's your name, mister?" He stopped in front of a young kid with cracked glasses and who looked as though he had lived on whipped cream and bonbons all his life.

"Frederick Hastings, sir."

"English?"

"Yes, sir. Greenwich, sir."

He wouldn't last more than three days, and it would be just as well to get rid of him. Foster wondered what kind of childish romantic novels were being written about the Legion these days.

The next man was a giant. The Russian, probably, and probably illiterate and stupid. He would make a good target for the Arabs. Next to him was the gypsy.

The man was staring straight ahead, his chin tucked in, his shoulders back, and the trace of a smile on his face. Foster gazed at him for a full half-minute and moved on. When he had completed the line he moved to the front again where Lieutenant Fontaine and Sergeant Triand were standing at attention.

"Dismiss the first company, lieutenant."

Those were the veterans, and the lieutenant barked out the orders, commanding them to attention and then dismissing them. After they had moved off to the barracks, Foster gazed sourly at the recruits.

"You men are now members of the Foreign Legion. You have enlisted for five years, and you will serve for five years. You have made a contract and you will honor it.

"Every man will think of running away. Some of you will try it. None has ever succeeded. If the Legion does not get you, the Arabs will. If the Arabs don't get you, the desert will. I cannot advise you which will be most painful."

He knew the words meant little to them, and that in the next few months the heads of two or three of them would be delivered to the fort by Arabs looking for a reward. Another two or three would be found on the desert, and an equal number would be captured by the Legion and shot. Out of the hundred and eight of them, the Legion would get fifty or sixty good soldiers.

Foster looked them over again, noting that three or four were beginning to sway back and forth, on the verge of fainting. "Carry on, lieutenant," he said and strode off toward his office.

He had not been pleased with the situation when they arrived at Fort Bousaada. There were only twenty-two men garrisoned there under the command of a sergeant, and the place looked more like an Arab brothel than a military post.

When the war in Europe started, several of the outlying forts had been abandoned, while others were cut down to a minimum in order to send men to France. Bousaada was one of the latter, with only seventy-five men and one officer left to hold it. Then, when the two archaeologists came and fifty of the men were ordered to accompany them to Erfoud, it left only a skeleton garrison at the fort. That meant they could form no relief column in case Lieutenant Fontaine was attacked at the excavation site.

El Krim was doubtless aware of that fact. The irritating part of it was that Foster would soon be in the same position. According to the orders Colonel Dechamps had given him, all of the men he had brought were to go to Erfoud to protect Marneau at the excavation. As to increasing the size of the garrison at Bousaada and having a relief column available, Dechamps assured Foster that he would make every effort to requisition more men, and he would try to have them there within six or eight weeks. Which meant three or four months, if they were lucky.

Lieutenant Fontaine, the only survivor of the Erfoud massacre was in the infirmary and scheduled for transport back to the hospital in Oran when Foster arrived the night before. But the lieutenant had volunteered to return to duty, insisting that his wound was sufficiently healed.

"You understand, lieutenant, that our situation will be very much like the one you faced ten days ago. If El Krim decides to attack in force, our chances will be slim. Under such circumstances, I do not want you there unless you are fully capable of performing your duties. If you are not, it would be better for you to go to the hospital in Oran, or remain here in command of the fort."

"If El Krim is likely to attack, I would like to return to the excavation, sir."

Foster was not convinced of Fontaine's recovery. He looked pale and weak, and the scar across his cheek was still puffed and red. But it was the hazy look in his eyes that gave Foster some doubts. Fontaine had survived, but sometimes such experiences left deeper scars on men. Foster had seen it in France when wounded men returned to the front and then froze the next time they went into battle. On the other hand, with the shortage of veterans and no other junior officers, Foster could certainly use him.

"Very well, we will see, lieutenant. Now tell me about the attack."

There had been no clear warning, Fontaine told him. Arab scouts were observed two or three days in advance, and then El Krim came in force with five hundred mounted warriors and six or seven hundred on foot. It was over quickly, and then the Arabs had taken the archaeologists and gathered all the weapons and ammunition and left.

"Did they get the machine gun?"

"No, sir. The men had orders to render it inoperable if the situation appeared hopeless. Corporal Hoffman did so."

"Good," Foster said. El Krim's getting fifty or sixty good rifles was bad enough. Then Fontaine told him about his escape.

He had lain in the latrine for twenty-four hours, unconscious from lack of blood a good part of the time. Then he had seen a camel caravan stop briefly while a couple of Arabs looked over the carnage. But he didn't risk revealing himself. He had found some emergency rations, and taking as much water as he could carry, he had headed out across the desert traveling by night and sleeping by day.

From what Foster had observed so far, Fontaine seemed like a capable officer. Foster had the men up before dawn cleaning up the four-year accumulation of dust and sand in the barracks, and then he had started their training immediately.

When he left the parade ground, Foster went directly to the telegraph office, which was as cluttered and dirty as the rest of the fort. The corporal took his feet off the desk and a pipe out of his mouth and snapped to attention.

"How long have you been in the Legion, corporal?" Foster asked, glancing around.

"Eight years and four months, sir."

"And in all that time you have not learned that offices are kept clean and all papers are properly filed and not left on desks and tables?"

The man smiled hesitantly and shrugged. "Well, sir, Sergeant Boullez never—"

"Sergeant Boullez is now a corporal, mister, and if this place is not cleaned and shining in thirty minutes, you will no longer be a corporal."

"Yes, sir."

"Did you send the messages Sergeant Triand gave you last night?"

"Yes, sir, and a reply just came in." He tore a sheet of paper from a pad and handed it across the counter.

Request for Lt. Fontaine's return to active duty—approved. Request for issuance of travel vouchers for Mme. Picard return to Paris—approved.

Foster folded the paper and gave the corporal a narrow look. "You now have twenty-eight minutes to get this place cleaned up, mister."

Outside, Foster buttoned the message into his pocket and headed for the gate, not looking forward to what he had to do. If Madame Picard was in tears, or unreasonable about things, it would be awkward. But with the vouchers, she could leave Bousaada on the next train, and then register all her complaints in Marseilles or Paris.

The fort at Bousaada had been constructed in 1910, two years before France officially took over Morocco as a protectorate. At the time there was nothing more than a few dozen pink stucco hovels and a few palm trees. But soldiers meant money, and money meant commerce. Within two years, there were several thousand Arabs and a complete city built outside the walls of the fort. Being more or less on the caravan route from Timbuktu to the Barbary coast, there was also camel traffic from the Sahara, and a good many Berber tribesmen came down from the Atlas Mountains to do their trading. With open desert in all directions, the inhabitants of Bousaada still packed themselves like sardines into the bazaars and narrow streets; the shouting and dickering, and the braying donkeys and rattling carts, was deafening.

Foster picked his way through the crowds, ignoring the beggars and hawkers, and the merchants who held out jewelry and leather goods and bolts of cloth. He squeezed past a donkey cart loaded with charcoal and then angled off toward a narrow street that would take him to Bousaada's only hotel.

"Major Foster!"

It was a familiar voice—one that Foster hoped he would not hear again in Bousaada. He stopped abruptly and turned, his jaw clenched.

The man coming toward him was wearing a djellaba, but he probably had as much French and Spanish blood as anything else, and at some time or another he had probably been deported from every country surrounding the Mediterranean. His name was Leon, and among other things he operated Bousaada's only café and nightclub. The other things included a hip-pocket pawnshop, pimping, gunrunning, hashish dealing, and any other activity that would earn him a half franc without doing any work.

"I knew you would be back, major," he said grinning as he hurried over. He knew better than to extend his hand. "I knew nothing could kill Major Foster."

"Something can," Foster said and continued walking.

"What is that, major?"

"The guns you've been selling to El Krim."

"To El Krim? Ahhh, you mean those old antiques. They were junk, major. Old muskets I picked up in Spanish Morocco."

Foster turned sharply on him. "Did you know that fifty men were killed at Erfoud less than two weeks ago? How many of those do you think were killed with your rifles?"

Leon stepped back, then smiled sadly. "I was most distressed to hear of the incident, major. Believe me." He gave Foster a look of innocence and lifted his hands. "Had I known El Krim intended to—"

"You sell El Krim anything that shoots, and I'll kill you, Leon. Do you understand?"

"Yes, yes, of course."

Foster turned abruptly and walked away, but he could hear Leon rustling along behind him.

"She is not at the hotel, major."

Foster stopped again and looked at the greasy, smiling face. Leon pointed at an arched doorway two or three houses farther along the street. "She is in there, major. Room number twenty, upstairs."

Foster strode along the street and went through

the arch, both surprised and irritated by Leon's knowledge of his business. Very likely the man had the
telegraph wires tapped and knew everything that was
going on in the fort.

It was a shabby neighborhood. The courtyard
behind the arch was overgrown with weeds, and a few
half-dressed Arab children were playing in a corner.
He went up the stairs to a balcony and found the room
at the back of the building. He knocked sharply and
waited, looking back into the patio.

He hadn't noticed her when he came in, but there
was a woman sitting in the corner just inside the en-
trance. Standing next to her in an apartment door, a
young Arab girl—obviously a prostitute—was smiling
up at him. Then Madame Picard's voice came from
behind.

"What is it, major?"

The door was open only a few inches, but he
could see that her face was tired and strained. He
touched his hat. "It will take only a moment, madame."

She moved away, leaving the door open. Foster
stepped hesitantly inside, stopping a few feet from the
door.

The place was sparsely furnished; little more than
four walls and a tiled floor, with a small window on the
far side. Opposite the bed a kerosene stove and a half-
empty bottle of cognac stood on a rough table.

"If you have come to apologize, major, you are
wasting your time."

"I have not come to apologize, madame."

She was sitting on the bed, legs crossed, lighting a
cigarette. She gave him an indifferent glance and took
a deep breath. "My father was an archaeologist and
art historian, major. He looked at beauty with his eyes
and explained it with his tongue. Without those I am
sure he would not have wanted to live. Would you care
for a drink?"

It was not a friendly invitation. "No, thank you,
madame. I wished to inquire about your arrangements.
I presume your husband—"

"My husband is buried in a military cemetery
somewhere in France, major."

Foster nodded. He was surprised, but not particularly moved by the statement. Millions of husbands were buried in military cemeteries. Still, he felt himself oddly sympathetic and attracted to the woman as he stared at her.

"You were saying, major?"

"Yes," he said. "I had thought that . . . I have made arrangements for you to return to Paris, madame. If you will come to my office, I will issue transport vouchers enabling you to leave on the morning train."

"Don't bother, major," she said, "There is nothing for me in Paris."

"There is less for you here, madame."

She gave him a sardonic smile and rubbed out her cigarette. "I hardly think you are the one to judge that, major."

"The Arab women will have nothing to do with you. And Arab men have little regard for the niceties you may have become accustomed to in Parisian society. I would strongly advise you to leave as quickly as possible."

"Major, I am sure you felt it was your duty to come here and offer your good offices to help me return to Paris. But I have no desire to accept your offer. Now that you have been a good soldier and done your duty, I don't think we have anything more to talk about." She lifted her head and gazed evenly at him, her eyes smoldering with cool contempt. Then she rose and moved to the table. "Good day, major."

Foster watched her pour cognac into a glass tumbler. He felt he should say something more, but for the first time in his life, he seemed to be at a loss for words. He felt no guilt over her father's death, and he felt no obligation to help her in any way. But he still felt the need to say something, to communicate with her in some way. He also felt that he was somehow incapable of it.

After she sipped the drink, she gave him a questioning look, as if asking what the hell he was still doing there. He quickly touched his hat. "Good day, madame."

When he reached the bottom of the stairs, Leon was suddenly in front of him, half-bowing, gesturing toward the woman sitting in the corner. "Have you met Madame Vorneau, major?" he asked with a broad smile.

Three Arab girls were now leaning against the wall, smiling at him. Foster stared at the woman and the girls and then brushed Leon aside, almost knocking him down as he strode out through the arch. He walked rapidly up the street and back through the bazaar, paying no attention to the noise and the crowds, trying to blot out the last ten minutes from his mind.

It made no difference to him what the woman did. She was a fool to stay in Bousaada, and living in a neighborhood and an apartment like that, she would be raped or murdered or kidnapped and made a slave or some tribal chief's concubine within a matter of days. And then she would expect the Legion to come and rescue her.

At the fort he went to his quarters overlooking the parade grounds and poured himself a drink, cursing all archaeologists and art historians, and anybody else who had anything to do with the Louvre. He quickly downed it and then stood out on the balcony where he could see the snow-capped Atlas Mountains far across the desert.

He wished to hell the recruits were already trained and could march for Erfoud the first thing in the morning. He understood El Krim, and El Krim understood him. As far as he was concerned, the sooner they got it over with, the better.

VII

"Francois Gilbert! Occupation?"

"Ex-soldier."

"Ex-soldier, *what?*"

"Ex-soldier, sir!"

"Your number is two-six-eight-eight-nine. Never forget it. Henry Gage! Occupation?"

There were ten or twelve ex-soldiers, some truck drivers, bartenders, students, farmers, factory workers, salesmen, shopkeepers and unemployed.

"Marco Segrain! Occupation?"

"No questions are asked in the Legion, sir."

Lieutenant Fontaine's eyes lifted slowly from the clipboard. "Occupation?" he asked again.

"Premier of France, sir."

The clipboard came across in a backhanded swing, cracking solidly into Marco's teeth. It felt like a crowbar.

Fontaine didn't even pause. "Your number is two-six-eight-nine-two. Never forget it. Hans Eberhard! Occupation?"

Marco smiled to himself as he felt the blood trickle down his chin. He should have said "King of Siam." The lieutenant probably would have believed him.

"What the hell is that?!" Fontaine barked out a minute later.

"It's my hat, sir," Top-hat answered.

"Bring it here."

Top-hat got the silk hat from the shelf above his

bed and handed it over. The lieutenant smashed his fist through the top and flung the hat on the floor.

"Hans Oberg! Occupation?"

None of it made any sense. It was as if the sole objective of Fontaine and all his noncoms was to kill or maim every recruit in the fort. When they did push-ups, their hands were kicked out from under them. When they marched, the corporals strode up and down the column driving rifle butts into ribs and stomachs and heads. If a man fell, he was kicked until he got himself back in file. If a man didn't hold his rifle correctly at target practice, he got his face jammed into the breech with the heel of a boot. If he missed the target, he got a handful of sand thrown in his eyes— and then he was kicked in the head if he didn't hit the target with the next shot.

From an hour before dawn until nine at night, they were moving constantly, being battered and beaten from all sides. Then, an hour after they collapsed on their beds, Fontaine or one of the corporals was likely to be screaming at them to wake up and scrub the floors and clean the barracks windows. When it was done, they were ordered to stand at attention for another hour while they were told what shits they were. Then the beating and kicking started all over again when men dropped to the floor in a dead sleep.

Whether it was because he said he was the premier of France, or because he danced with Simone on the ship, Marco didn't know; but there was no doubt that he was getting special attention. A big muscular corporal with a handlebar moustache was constantly at his side, and along with the same bruises as everybody else Marco had three loose teeth and at least two cracked ribs before the second day was over.

"How do you like the Legion, gypsy?" the corporal asked him a hundred times.

"I love it, sir," Marco said. "Especially the corporals."

For that he would get a fist in the face, or the ear, or in the ribs. "The Legion hates gypsies, soldier."

"So do I, corporal. Some of my worst enemies are gypsies."

He would be staggered by another blow, and the man would glower at him with their noses almost touching and the smell of sour wine heavy in Marco's face. "The Legion hates smart-asses, soldier. How do you like the Legion?"

"Love it, sir."

"The Legion hates liars, soldier. Get your pack and run around the perimeter of the compound forty times."

"Thank you, sir," Marco said the third time it happened. "By the way, it's my duty to tell you, sir, there's a lot of talk in the barracks about you and me."

"What the hell are you talking about?"

"Well, sir, everybody says you're crazy about dark-haired gypsies."

That's when Marco got his teeth loosened and his ribs cracked. Then he ran around the perimeter eighty times while everybody else ate dinner and staggered off to their cots.

At first it seemed as if it was all a ritual, like some kind of initiation ceremony that would only last a day or two. But Marco finally realized there was more to it than that. There was a deep bitterness in most of the noncoms; an attitude of resentment over the belief that while they had been suffering through years of misery and privation in the Legion, all the recruits had been enjoying the comforts and pleasures of civilized life. So it was a matter of balancing the score, and in the two or three weeks of training making sure that every recruit paid up in full for his years of pleasure and self-indulgence. If a man did well at target practice or marched all day without tiring, the resentment was even greater; and if a man smiled or laughed, it was like spitting on the scars and infirmities of a twenty-year veteran. It was not an initiation, and it was not going to end in two days.

On the third night, Marco thought he was dreaming when he felt a hand on his shoulder. He was sleeping face-down on his bed, one arm dangling over the side, and his body too stiff and sore to roll over. Then the hand was shaking him, stirring him from deep sleep into half-consciousness. He was on the Riviera, and the heavy snoring around him was the sound of waves rolling gently up on the sand.

"Marco!" a voice hissed. The hand shook him again and he shifted his head to the other side.

Top-hat was kneeling next to his cot, frowning at him. "What's the matter?" Marco groaned. He lifted himself painfully to an elbow.

"I've gotta talk to you."

Marco took a deep breath and rubbed his eyes. A little moonlight was coming through the windows, but he and Top-hat seemed to be the only ones awake. "What time is it?"

"It's about two o'clock. Let's go down to the latrine."

There was a note of urgency, or worry—or was it fear?—in Top-hat's voice. Marco blinked a couple times and finally nodded.

It was cold, and Marco pulled the blanket off his cot, sliding it over his shoulders as he followed Top-hat past the lines of snoring men and then the corporal's room. In the latrine they both sat on benches and Top-hat offered a cigarette.

"I'm going to desert, Marco," he said after the cigarettes were lit.

Marco was only a little surprised. Top-hat had probably been kicked and battered and cursed more than any man in the company, and he was probably in the worst shape to take it. The last two mornings, Marco had to lift him out of bed to get him started. But Marco doubted if he was serious about deserting.

"How do you plan to do it?" he asked quietly.

"At night. I think that's the best time. If I'm lucky maybe there'll be some clouds to block out the moon tomorrow night. The gates are locked, but I don't think it'll be too much trouble getting over the wall."

Marco took a puff on the cigarette and gave him a closer look, wondering if he was wrong about how serious the man was. Top-hat was squinting thoughtfully at the floor.

"And then what?"

"I don't know for sure. Maybe just head out across the desert. Or maybe I can hide somewhere on the train before it leaves."

"I don't think you'd have much chance hiding on the train. If a man was missing, it'd be the first place they'd search."

"Okay, then it'll have to be the desert. It probably won't be too hard to steal a camel somewhere in town."

"Have you ever ridden a camel?"

"No, but I noticed they've got saddles on them. And they gallop along pretty fast. If I got an early start, I figure I could be thirty or forty miles away before they even noticed I was gone. And I'll take food and water along, of course."

Marco gazed at his cigarette and then off at the corner of the room. "What did you do before you joined the Legion, Top-hat?"

"I'm a piano player. I played in bars and night-clubs. Anyplace."

"Why did you join the Legion?"

Top-hat shrugged and dropped his cigarette to the floor. "I don't know. Why does a man do anything? I became a piano player because it was easy and I could make a living at it. So all through the war I played for the soldiers coming to Paris on leave. I entertained them and they went back and died."

"You were never in the army?"

"No, they didn't want me." He gave Marco a hesitant glance and laughed. "I had tuberculosis once. Strange, isn't it? All the healthy, virile young men were turned into cannon fodder, and I was protected from it. People like me should have been the first to go. My brother was killed the third day of the war."

"So you joined the Legion to make up for that?"

He shrugged. "No questions asked."

Marco had a feeling that Top-hat hadn't told him the whole story of why he joined the Legion. But whatever the reason it had been a big mistake. Now he was suffering worse agonies than those he had tried to leave behind. He was like a man who hated and feared water all his life and never learned to swim, then jumped into the middle of the ocean hoping the one courageous act would straighten out all his problems.

"I don't think you ought to try to escape," Marco said.

Top-hat gazed at him for a minute and got out another cigarette. "Do you know who those two men in the baskets were the other day? The ones Major Foster shot?"

"No."

"They were archaeologists and art historians from the Louvre. The Arabs took them prisoner when they raided an excavation in a place called Erfoud, about forty miles from here. That's the same place Lieutenant Fontaine got all cut up. And do you know why they're trying to get us trained so fast?"

"No," Marco said. He didn't realize their training was any different from usual.

"They're doing it because three more archaeologists from the Louvre want to go to Erfoud, and we're going along to fight off the Arabs. The last ones were attacked by twelve hundred men, and now we're going to get slaughtered the same way."

Marco was silent for a minute, thinking about their chances in a battle with twelve hundred Arabs. He supposed the Legionnaires were better at fighting and had bigger and better guns. But he wondered about six-to-one odds.

"We haven't got one chance in a thousand if we go out there, Marco. At least if we go over the wall, we could make a decent try at it. And with two of us, the chances would be a lot better."

That was the first Top-hat had said anything about Marco going along, and Marco glanced at him, a little surprised. Since their train ride down from Oran, the only time he had thought about deserting was when Major Foster made his little speech telling how nobody had ever successfully run away from the Legion. Marco had done a lot of things people didn't think could be done, and the major's challenge stirred some interest in him. But since they had been in Bousaada, things had moved too fast, and he had been too tired to give the matter any more thought.

Getting over the wall would be no problem, even with Top-hat along. From that point on, he wasn't so sure. Stealing camels might bring a fast alarm, and not speaking Arabic could cause more problems once they got out on the desert. They could steal djellabas and burnooses along with the camels, and maybe they could pass for Arabs. Then what? Pretend they were holy men under a vow of silence? And what direction could they go? North, along the railroad tracks would be the worst, and south or east into several thousand miles of empty Sahara desert would be just as bad. So that left west, toward Marrakesh. Which meant going through the Atlas Mountains, where the most ferocious of the Berber tribesmen were supposed to be.

No, Marco decided. In Oran or Oujda, or any of the towns near the coast, it might be possible to slip away and find a boat within a few hours. But the chance of beating the desert and the Arabs and the Legion all at once was pretty remote.

"Have you mentioned this to anybody else?"

"No. I thought I'd talk to you first. But I know Eberhard and Schmidt have been talking about deserting, too."

Marco smiled. They were a couple of thick-headed Germans who would probably break their legs trying to get over the wall.

"There is also the possibility of our getting some outside help," Top-hat said. "Someone to get us camels and some different clothes."

Marco frowned. "How?"

"Have you forgotten about Madame Picard?" Top-hat asked.

Marco had not forgotten about her, but he had some doubts about ever seeing her again. From what he had seen of the town of Bousaada, he couldn't imagine her hanging around the place very long. "You mean she's still here?"

"Yes. She has an apartment."

Marco was puzzled. "How did you find that out?"

"One of the veterans does a lot of business with a man in town named Leon. He told me."

"What's she doing here?"

Top-hat gave him a hesitant glance. "Her father was one of those men Major Foster shot out in the desert."

Oh, my God! Marco thought. And she had probably watched the whole thing from the train window. "How is she?"

Top-hat shrugged. "Apparently her apartment is in the bad part of town. I haven't heard how she is or what she's doing. Major Foster made arrangements for her to go back to Paris, but she refused to go. Do you think she would help us? In five more days we get to leave the fort at night. You could ask her then."

When Top-hat mentioned Simone, the subject of desertion had suddenly left Marco's mind. He blinked at Top-hat. "I don't know," he said. "I'm not sure I would even ask her, Top-hat."

Top-hat smiled sadly. "That's what I was afraid of."

"Listen, Top-hat, just take it one day at a time. You've made it through three days now, and every day'll be a little easier. You've survived today, and you can survive tomorrow."

"I can't, Marco. I can't do it."

"Try, Top-hat, try."

In the next five days, Marco switched positions with other recruits to be next to Top-hat and give him support when it looked as if he was going to drop. At target practice, he helped him with holding and positioning his rifle, and two or three times he fired across from the other end of the line and hit bull's-eyes in Top-hat's target to bring up his score. Big Ivan helped, silently stepping in when he was needed, and at the end of each day Top-hat collapsed wearily on his cot. On the morning of the fifth day Top-hat grabbed Marco's arm as they rolled out of bed.

"Tonight we get to go into town, Marco," he said. "Two camels, food and water, and Arab clothing is all we need."

Marco smiled and nodded. Then Lieutenant Fontaine was screaming at them, driving them out into the early-morning darkness and another day of hell.

"Ninety percent of the Arab women have syphilis or gonorrhea," Fontaine snarled as they stood at attention after dinner. "A good many of them have both. Any man not present and accounted for at the five A.M. roll call will automatically be considered a deserter and will be shot when he is found. Any man drunk at the five A.M. roll call will be secured to a stake on the parade ground and left all day to sober up in the sun. Any man molesting any Arab or otherwise disturbing the peace in Bousaada will spend two days in the punishment cell without food or water. Company attention! Company dismissed!"

Outside the gate they were met by a mob of peddlers offering everything from gold bracelets and hashish to pickled watermelon rind and twelve-year-old cognac fresh out of the bathtub. Marco smiled as he pushed his way through with Top-hat and Ivan and Fred. It reminded him of a gypsy carnival, or the mobs of people who used to pour into the Paris circus years ago. Except that *he* was the "mark" now and the *Arabs* were the carnies.

Leon's café was the only place to go, the veteran legionnaire named Andre told them. He led the way, waving off the peddlers and moving down through the bazaar and the smells of incense and potent perfumes.

"You want a girl, soldier?" a small boy said, hanging onto Marco's sleeve. "Nice English girl? French? Any kind you want. All virgins."

"How do you know they're virgins?" Marco asked.

"Guaranteed," the boy said with a serious frown. "Just arrived from Marrakesh. Money back if you're not satisfied."

Marco laughed and waved the boy off. "Maybe later."

"Later they won't be virgins!" the boy yelled and headed for another group of legionnaires.

It looked as if every legionnaire from the fort was

at Leon's. It was a tacky-looking place with Moorish arches surrounding a tiled dance floor. Half of the plaster had dropped from the walls, and the tapestries and chairs and tables all looked as if they had been picked up from a rubbish heap.

"Welcome, welcome," a greasy man said, bowing at the door as they filed in behind a few dozen other legionnaires. He was dressed in a cheap pinstriped suit and looked like a mixture of all the races in the world.

"Are you Mr. Leon?" Marco asked.

"Just Leon," the man smiled.

"Okay, Leon, we'd like a quiet window-table for five with candlelight and close to the floor show."

The man gaped at him. "A window-table, sir?"

Marco gave him a pat on the shoulder and moved on. "It's all right, Leon, we'll manage by ourselves."

The bar along the right side was three-deep with legionnaires, and most of the tables were already occupied. Andre led them across the dance floor and found an empty one close to the wall and then signaled the waitress for wine. After the bottle was delivered, Marco noticed Major Foster sitting at a table across the room.

He was a sad-looking man, Marco decided. He was sitting alone with a bottle of Scotch whiskey, gazing absently off at the bar. Probably thinking up new tortures for the recruits.

"Top-hat, why don't you play something for us?"

A battered piano stood next to the dance floor. Top-hat glanced over and nodded. "Are you going to talk to Madame Picard tonight?" he asked quietly.

"If I can find her."

"Her address is forty-two, rue Marrakesh, apartment twenty."

"Okay. I'll see if I can find her later."

Top-hat went to the piano and a dozen legionnaires quickly gathered around him as he started to play.

Ten minutes later, Andre ordered another bottle of wine. Ivan had emptied the first glass as if it were a thimble, and then he sat in silence, gazing broodingly around at the noisy legionnaires.

"Anything you want," Andre was telling them.
"All the girls in the place work for Leon, and there are
rooms up those stairs."

"Do they have diseases?" Fred asked with a sick
look.

"Leon claims they're all clean, but I wouldn't try
to sue him if you get a few warts."

Most of the girls were already sitting with legionnaires, giggling and asking for more drinks. At a table
near the dance floor, five or six were sitting by themselves, smiling at anybody who would smile back.
They looked like Arab girls, or maybe Berbers, but
they were wearing heavy makeup and Western dress
—short skirts with blouses buttoned low to give a good
view of the merchandise. They were probably from
Marrakesh or Fez or small mountain towns, and after
they earned some money they would return home all
wrapped up in djellabas and veils and be married off
as unseen and untouched virgins.

Leon was moving among the tables now, talking
to legionnaires. "Ahhh, my good friend, Andre," he
said as he reached their table. "Do you have anything
for me? Some nice jewelry from Oran? Or you would
like to buy some fine gold, maybe?"

Andre snorted. "You took everything I ever had
years ago, Leon. Maybe you can do some business with
my gypsy friend here."

Leon smiled when he looked at Marco. "Ah, your
table is satisfactory, sir? And perhaps I can show you
some fine gold rings from Tangier?"

"I don't buy, I sell," Marco said.

"Then we can do business one day, my friend.
You can always find me here."

"He's the richest man in Bousaada," Andre said
after Leon moved off. "And the slimiest. He owns half
the legionnaires in Morocco."

Marco watched the man scrape and bow his way
among the tables showing his bits of gold and jewelry.
Then Leon suddenly straightened and moved hurriedly
across the room.

Marco blinked, not quite believing it. Simone was
coming through the door.

"Look, Marco," Fred said, pointing.

"I see."

Leon was smiling and bowing, leading her off to a roped-off table at the side. He drew her chair out and hovered at her shoulder as she sat down. Then he snapped his fingers and called for champagne.

She was more beautiful than ever, and everybody in the place—including Major Foster—was looking at her. She seemed indifferent to all the attention, and a little bored as Leon sat close and grinned and gestured while he talked to her.

"Excuse me, gentlemen," Marco said and pushed his chair back.

"Be careful," Andre warned, "Leon has a long memory."

Marco smiled. "So do I." He moved around the tables and along the wall, coming in quietly behind Simone.

Leon had poured the champagne and was almost drooling as he lifted his glass. "To you, Madame Picard, and to a long friendship."

Marco heard her laugh softly as she lifted her glass. "You expect a great deal for the price of champagne, monsieur."

"Leon," Marco said, moving forward, "perhaps we can do some business after all."

Simone looked up and Marco smiled. "Excuse me for the interruption, madame." He eased into a chair and brought Simone's earrings from his pocket. "A very valuable pair of earrings, Monsieur Leon. Perhaps you would be interested?"

"Oh, they are very beautiful, monsieur," Simone exclaimed.

Marco smiled at her. "You like them, madame? I thought you might. I secured them from a lovely lady while I was traveling through Africa. Remarkable stones, don't you think?"

"Indeed. I think they would suit me very well."

Leon was looking from one of them to the other, his eyes widening. "Madame, allow me to make a gift of them to you." He smiled at Marco. "Forty francs."

"For stones like this?! You insult the lady, monsieur."

Simone was having difficulty controlling her smile. "I had a pair very much like these once," she said. "I was very fond of them."

"I'll give you sixty," Leon offered.

"Sixty? Ah, my friend, these are very special earrings. They once belonged to the most beautiful woman in the world. A princess. They are very valuable to me."

Simone gazed at him and then turned to Leon. "I want them," she purred.

"One hundred francs," Leon said firmly.

Marco frowned as if considering it, then shook his head.

"One hundred and fifty," Leon announced.

"No," Marco said, "I don't think I could sell them." He smiled at Simone. "However, madame, there is a way I might be persuaded to part with them."

"Oh?" Simone answered, "I would be very interested in hearing what it is."

"If you will come with me, madame?" Marco rose to draw out her chair, smiling at Leon. It looked as if the man's eyes were going to drop on the table. Simone rose, then stopped short as a gray-haired man suddenly appeared at Marco's elbow.

"Excuse me, Madame Picard," he said glancing uneasily at Marco and Leon. "Major Foster and I would like to invite you to join us for a drink, if you would be so kind."

Marco couldn't help glancing across the room at Foster. There were two other men at the table with him now, and he was glaring hard across the room.

"I am very sorry, Monsieur Marneau," Simone said coolly, "but we were just leaving."

Marneau gave Marco an icy glance, his voice suddenly more businesslike. "Then please be good enough to come to my office tomorrow, madame. I have some of your father's things."

Simone gave him a brief smile and then hooked her arm in Marco's as they moved toward the door. Marco avoided Foster's eyes, but he knew the major was watching, and that Simone's cheerful smile was for his benefit.

The courtyard outside was almost as crowded as the café, except that the legionnaires seemed to be drunker. Some were dancing, others sloppily embracing prostitutes, or dragging them off into the darkness.

"Sad, aren't they?" Marco said as they reached the gate and turned up the street.

"Which ones?" she asked.

Marco was surprised by the soft sadness of her tone. He had expected her to be laughing over Leon and the earrings. "All of them," he said.

"Well, at least they know their future," she said distantly.

Marco decided not to say anything as they walked. She guided them, her face expressionless as they passed through narrow cobblestoned alleys and finally turned through an arch into a courtyard. At the bottom of a stairway, she stopped and looked at him.

"You're wasting your time, Marco," she said softly.

He laughed. "Would it be better spent drinking wine in Leon's?"

"It might. I really have nothing to offer you. I'm not worth it, Marco."

Marco was confused by her tone and the sudden emptiness of her eyes. "I think you are more valuable than anything in the world to me."

"You are very much alive, and I am not. I am dead, and I think I grow more so every day."

"Your father was—"

"It's not just my father, Marco. I waited four years for a soldier to come home from the front. He was my husband, but he was killed, and now I am as dead as he is."

"You are mistaken, Simone. You are—"

She was shaking her head. "Everything I love dies, Marco."

Marco touched her chin and lifted it. "And everything I love comes alive. And life is stronger than death."

He kissed her softly on the forehead, then the cheeks, and drew her close. She was suddenly holding him tight, her head limp against his chest, crying softly.

VIII

According to Andre, they would march forty
miles—twenty miles directly east into the rising sun
and then twenty miles directly west into the afternoon
sun. Each man would carry a one-hundred-pound
pack—weighted with rocks, if necessary.

The first hour seemed the worst to Marco. Major
Foster had come down from his quarters as quickly as
the recruits formed the column. He gave them a single
hard look and then commanded them to march,
striding out briskly in front of them. From then on, his
pace didn't falter or vary a half inch or a half second
as they passed through the gates and headed into the
empty desert. It was a faster pace than Fontaine usually
maintained, and it seemed as if an entirely new set of
muscles were being stretched and tortured. Within ten
minutes, men were puffing and skipping to regain their
step, and the two corporals were snarling alongside,
threatening and kicking at those who drifted more
than an inch out of line.

The second hour seemed to be easier. A dull
numbness took over, and with eyes fixed on the kepi
bobbing along directly in front, a man could half-
close his eyes and shut out everything but the grunting
rhythm of boots and creaking leather.

An hour later, with the blinding sun halfway up,
Marco felt the first drops of perspiration skid down his
ribs and the warming sand began to burn through the
soles of his boots.

Top-hat was in the row just ahead, and two places
over, next to Ivan. Marco glanced at him occasionally,

seeing his head sag forward and then jerk back as he took deep breaths and pushed himself on.

It had been early morning and almost time for roll call when Marco returned to the barracks from Simone's apartment three nights earlier. Top-hat had been waiting, smoking cigarettes and pacing back and forth in the latrine. "What'd she say?" he asked as quickly as Marco came in.

"If you want to try it, you'll get everything you need."

Top-hat looked surprised and then grinned uncertainly. "She really said that? She'll get the camels?"

"You'll get one camel and whatever Arab clothing and food you want."

"Just one? You mean you're not going?"

"No," Marco told him.

It was a decision Marco had made while he walked back from Simone's apartment. He had kept Top-hat alive for five days, hoping that things would get easier for him and he would change his mind. Marco had no intention of deserting, and he felt guilty about leading Top-hat on. But he hadn't said a word to Simone about getting camels because he knew damned well that Top-hat would be killed in one way or another within twenty-four hours after he went over the wall.

So, if Top-hat was still crazy enough to want to try it, Marco had decided he would steal the camel himself. He would see that Top-hat got packed up and dressed and pointed in the right direction across the desert, and that would be the end of it.

Top-hat stared at him for a minute and sat down with his head in his hands. "I can't make it alone," he whimpered, almost in tears. "I'm no good at that sort of thing. Please go with me."

"You can make it, Top-hat."

"I can't. I don't think I can even ride a camel."

Marco sat down and put a hand on his shoulder. "I don't mean that. I mean you can make it in the Legion."

Top-hat shook his head.

"Listen," Marco said, "We all got into this not knowing what it was, and we're all in the same boat.

But someday you've got to stand up and face it, and you have to make a decision and stick to it, and see it through to the end no matter how much it hurts. So if you really think your chances are better going over the wall than at Erfoud, you've got to do it. And you've got to do it on your own and not depend on somebody else to take care of you. You could ride a camel if you wanted to. You could also become a legionnaire and be as good a soldier as anybody here. Just don't run from one fire and jump into a bigger one hoping some kind of miracle is going to save you. You know what I mean?"

Top-hat had finally leaned his head against the wall and nodded. "I know."

"Think about it," Marco had finally said. "If you want the camel, I'll get it for you. But make the decision yourself, Top-hat. That's the first step."

Marco hadn't bothered to undress. With roll call less than half an hour away, he lay on his cot and stared at the ceiling, wondering what the hell he was doing giving people advice about how to manage their lives. If he was so smart, he wouldn't be in the Legion himself. He also wouldn't be in love with a girl who kept telling him not to waste his time with her.

When they started the long march, Marco still had no idea what Top-hat had decided, or whether he had made any decision at all. After that night, neither of them mentioned it, and Top-hat had gone through two more days of Fontaine's tortures as if he were in a daze. Then he ate dinner and flopped on his bed with his head buried under his pillow. And now he was staggering along, glassy-eyed, squinting up at the sun every two minutes and taking another deep breath to carry him twenty more steps.

The worst parts were the sand dunes. Most of them were hard and crusted on one side and soft on the other. If a man had any sense, he could pick out a fairly reasonable course sticking to the harder surfaces. But Major Foster seemed completely unaware of such possibilities. He walked in a straight line directly east, and if it took them into the lowest part of the deepest gully, or over the highest peak of the tallest sand dune, that's where they went. Struggling up through the soft sand, men stumbled and sometimes slid back down on their faces. The corporals screamed and kicked at them until they hurried back into place, and then they all plodded on, lips cracking, the flinty sand thick in their nostrils and mouths and eyes, and somehow finding its way into their boots.

Marco felt some relief as he watched Top-hat. He was going to make it—at least to their break at the halfway point. His feet seemed to be stumbling over each other occasionally, but he wasn't falling. Then Marco saw why. Ivan's hand was in Top-hat's armpit. The big man was marching along easily, eyes front, back straight, almost lifting Top-hat off his feet.

Marco narrowed his eyes and plodded on, praying that Ivan's strength would keep up.

"Company, halt!" one of the corporals finally called out from the front of the column. They all stopped and stood shakily at attention, their legs not moving for the first time in five hours. "Company—fall out!"

They spread out, stumbling to the ground, pulling off packs, groaning and sighing. Marco helped as Ivan eased Top-hat slowly to the sand. Then he opened his canteen and held it to his mouth.

"Drink, Top-hat."

Fred poured some water into his cupped hand and splashed it in Top-hat's face.

He finally drank. Half of the water slopped down his chin and soaked into his already sweat-stained blouse. Then he gave them all a weak smile and eased down on his back. "I appreciate it," he mumbled and closed his eyes.

They were dead center in the middle of nowhere —a sizzling caldron of sand stretching off in endless ripples and waves in every direction. Marco pulled off his pack and lay down with his head resting on it and closed his eyes.

Each of them had been issued four ounces of cheese and twelve dates, but only Ivan seemed to have an appetite. He pushed all of the dates in his mouth at

once and chewed away at them, now and then spitting
a pit into the sand. After he finished the dates he
nudged Marco with an elbow and smiled across the
scattered group of legionnaires.

He was looking at Lieutenant Fontaine. During
the march the lieutenant had been in front of the column where they couldn't see him. Now he was slumped
in the sand, staring emptily off at nothing.

Marco smiled and nibbled at some cheese, looking
absently around for Major Foster. It was hard to imagine their great leader sitting or lying down, and apparently he wasn't. Marco twisted, looking behind him
and finally saw the small figure striding up the side of a
sand dune a mile farther to the east. "For Christ's sake,
look at that!" he said.

Even Top-hat twisted a little to squint across the
desert. The major was now standing on a high dune,
looking off to the south through a pair of field glasses.

"What do you suppose he's looking at?" Fred
asked.

Marco twisted farther, scanning the empty desert
to the south. Then he saw them—two pairs of mounted
Arabs standing like statues in the hazy sea of sand.

It was hard to tell how far away they were. In
the shimmering heat, it appeared to be less than a mile.
Then their heads and shoulders seemed to separate
from their bodies and they were no more than quivering and indistinct blots on the horizon. Marco squeezed
his eyes and blinked a couple of times and then gave
it up.

The major was coming back now, striding down
the side of the sand dune as if he were just starting
out on his morning constitutional. Lieutenant Fontaine
was also on his feet, apparently coming back to life
now that the major was returning.

Marco looked at Top-hat, studying the dust-caked
face and the tired eyes. "You can make it, Top-hat."

The eyes blinked and focused hazily.

Marco smiled at him. "Just pretend you're wearing your top hat and tails and you're walking down
the Champs-Élysées to the Ritz."

Top-hat smiled, then winced at the pain from his

cracked lips. "Do you still have Madame Picard's earrings, Marco?"

Marco frowned at him, surprised by the strange question. "Yes," he said.

"Be careful," Top-hat mumbled. "I meant to tell you before. That night in Leon's, I heard Corporal Laplanche talking about them. He was telling some other legionnaires that Leon offered him a lot of money if he could steal them from you."

Marco frowned and glanced off at Corporal Laplanche. Up until now he hadn't paid much attention to Laplanche. The corporal was a giant-sized brute, no more or less sadistic than some of the other noncoms. But Marco had sensed a sly and cunning side to the man, and he had avoided him as much as he could. He did precisely what the corporal ordered, and didn't waste any smiles or smart remarks on him.

To his surprise, Marco saw the corporal gazing back at him from the far side of the group. He was sitting by himself, an arm resting across his propped-up knee, finishing off the last of his dates. Marco smiled, then dropped his head to his pack and closed his eyes again.

It was interesting, he reflected. Leon and Corporal Laplanche figured he still had the earrings. After his and Simone's performance in the café, it would seem reasonable that the earrings were now in her possession. So they were either stupid, or else they figured Simone had not fulfilled her part of the bargain. He smiled, deciding it was both. Laplanche was stupid, and Leon would find it impossible to believe a woman like Simone could give herself to a lowly recruit for a pair of earrings.

"Levez-vous! Levez-vous!" Laplanche was bawling out while he strode among the men. Foster was staring down at them from a sand dune, his feet apart and his hands behind him as if he had been waiting impatiently all day.

"Par files de quarte!" Laplanche commanded.

They re-formed the column and Marco squeezed in beside Top-hat, telling the other man to take his place in the rank behind. The man shrugged and moved back.

Foster was striding to the front and the corporal took his position at the side. *"En avant! Marche!"*

The agony came more quickly now. In the first five minutes, their stiffened legs became limber again, and they fell easily into the monotonous rhythm. But within half an hour, the heat and pain and weariness came back with compounded vengeance. Even the two corporals were now less energetic about patrolling the ranks. They slogged along at the flanks thirty yards ahead, glancing back only occasionally to see that everyone was keeping pace. But far out ahead of the column Major Foster was still breezing along, striding up and over sand dunes, his eyes fixed unerringly on some compass point a thousand miles ahead.

An hour later, Top-hat was suddenly gone.

Both Ivan and Marco had watched him closely at first. He seemed to be doing much better than before, even smiling occasionally. Then Marco's thoughts had finally drifted into a numbed and endless counting of the one-two-three-four cadence. Then there were sudden grunts and a broken rhythm in the footsteps behind, and Marco realized that Top-hat was no longer beside him.

Ivan turned at the same time, both of them hurrying back and grabbing an arm, hoisting Top-hat to his feet again.

"In file! In file!" Laplanche was yelling as he strode toward them. By then they had Top-hat back in position and the ranks had re-formed behind them. He was marching again, blinking hazily ahead.

The corporal marched alongside, watching for a minute and then moved forward again. Marco and Ivan grabbed Top-hat's arms. His chin dropped to his chest and his legs were hardly moving. "It's no use," he said thickly, "It's too far to the Ritz, Marco."

"It's okay, Top-hat, you're gonna make it."

After ten more minutes Marco felt his grip loosening. He grabbed Top-hat's arm with his left hand and lifted, attempting to get his other hand deeper into the armpit. Then Top-hat was gone again, sprawling face-down with Ivan trying to hang onto the other arm.

The men in the three ranks behind split and marched around them, a few glancing back as they re-formed behind the column.

They hoisted him to his feet again, but Top-hat made no effort to move his legs or stand. Marco shifted, getting his arm firmly under Top-hat's and then he stopped short, staring off to the side.

Major Foster was standing on a dune ten yards away, glaring at them. "Leave that man alone, soldier!"

Ivan frowned and looked at Marco.

"In the Legion, you march or die, mister! Get his pack and rifle! Now!"

Marco stared at the hard, narrowed eyes and the flexing jaw, not believing the man could be serious. Nobody could be that stupid, or cruel, or so dedicated to something as asinine as the Legion's code of discipline. Top-hat was completely limp, probably unaware of what was going on. Ivan stared at Marco as if waiting for instructions.

Marco eased Top-hat back to the ground, working his pack loose from his shoulders. On the other side, Ivan did the same, then picked up Top-hat's rifle.

"Back in the ranks—double-time!" Foster barked.

Marco hesitated as Ivan moved off. "We can carry the man, sir. If we leave him here—"

Marco saw the face redden as the jaws clamped tight. "Do you know what it means to disobey an officer in the Legion, mister? You've got two seconds to get back in the column!"

Marco quickly shifted Top-hat's kepi so the rim would shade his face. Then he headed out after Ivan, jogging at double-speed.

"You son-of-a-bitch!" he said softly between his teeth. "You crazy fucking madman!"

He gave a final backward glance as he moved into position. All he could see of Top-hat was a motionless heap curled up between two sand dunes. The major was coming along, steadily catching up, his eyes once again fixed on that point dead ahead. A minute later he was striding past, not even giving them a glance as he moved to the front.

Top-hat's pack was surprisingly light; no more than twenty pounds. Marco looked at it, then saw why. Ivan's pack was bulging on all sides, the tie strings barely holding it together. Ivan must have transferred everything while they ate lunch.

"Can you carry this?" Marco asked the Russian. He handed the pack over, and Ivan took it without hesitating. Then Marco edged around behind Ivan and took the outside position where he could see ahead.

They were moving down the broad slope of a sand dune, the men in the front ranks already starting up the slope of the next one. On the flanks the corporals were not even glancing back now. Marco waited until a large dune came and they were going up. Then, just before the crest, he stepped to the side and stopped, letting the three ranks march past him. When they were over the crest, he dropped quickly to his hands and knees and watched as the column marched on, moving up and over the next dune. Five minutes later, they were almost out of sight—a tiny column of ants appearing and then disappearing as they went up and over the sand dunes.

There was no problem following the broad path of churned sand back, and Marco strode rapidly up and down the drifts thinking about Top-hat, and how maybe it would have been better if he had gotten him a camel and let him go over the wall. He probably would have died just as fast, but at least he would have had the satisfaction of having tried to beat the Legion.

Glancing ahead Marco saw two gray-brown lumps rising slightly above the level of the dunes and he strode on, blinking to clear his eyes. Then, cresting the next slope, he stopped dead in his tracks.

Less than a hundred feet ahead, just beyond the next dune, he could see the heads and humps of two camels standing side by side, their saddles empty. Was it the spot where they had left Top-hat? It had to be!

Marco moved quickly down the slope and almost to the crest of the next one, dropping to his belly as he slithered the last twenty feet. He could see them—two Arabs in faded blue djellabas, hovering over Top-hat. But Top-hat seemed to be conscious and unhurt. His arm was moving, feebly brushing at the Arabs' hands as they went through his pockets. They looked like two vultures picking at a half-dead carcass.

Marco drew his bayonet from the scabbard and fixed it to the end of his rifle. Christ, he thought, had all those things Fontaine had been teaching them about hand-to-hand fighting been worth a damn? Or would he be better off just shooting the bastards?

He quickly gave up that idea when he scanned the horizon to the south and behind him. About a mile and a half away, moving along at a parallel with the column of legionnaires, were two more mounted Arabs. If he fired any shots, they would be galloping back at full speed. The rifle balanced in his right hand, Marco edged higher on the dune and came to his feet, hesitating a moment. Then, bellowing out the loudest, most blood-curdling scream he could manage, he raced down the slope, the bayonet flying like an unleashed arrow at the midsection of the closest Arab.

He saw the man turn, and for an instant a bearded face gaped at him. Then the blade was piercing through cloth and flesh, driving the man backwards and off his feet with the impact. The rifle twisted, turning downward as the man hit the sand, and Marco half-stumbled as he whirled and yanked the blade out.

The second man had run, and he was already in the saddle, lifting a long sword as the animal wobbled and came to its feet. Marco charged again, screaming, holding the rifle high, leveled at the Arab's belly. Then he was knocked to the side as the camel suddenly pivoted, blocking his attack. He moved to the right, then ducked under the animal's neck, ducking again as the heavy sword flashed across two inches above his head.

His next move was mostly from instinct—from years of experience at alley fighting when he was a boy in Granada. With the man leaning forward, his weight off center from the missed swing, Marco instantly grabbed at the wrist, jerking it forward, toppling the man from the saddle. Then he had one foot clamping the man's wrist to the ground and the tip of the bayonet touching the man's neck just above the breastbone.

"Enshallah," the man breathed, staring wide-eyed at him.

"Enshallah to you, too," Marco grunted and jammed the rifle forward, popping the blade through the windpipe.

It was over. For a minute Marco gazed stiffly down at the man's face, breathing heavily, watching the blood bubble slowly from the severed throat. When he finally drew the blade out he staggered across to Top-hat and dropped to the sand, too exhausted to speak.

Top-hat was sitting up now, frowning at the dead Arab as if wondering why the man was there. Then he squinted off at the two camels. They were already over the crest of the dune, picking up speed as they galloped away.

Fifty yards ahead of the column, Major Foster angled off to the left as they approached the open gates of the fort. Then he stationed himself to the side as he watched the others draw closer.

They had done better than he had expected— only one man down. But he gave Lieutenant Fontaine a close look as the lieutenant marched by. The man had done a good job conditioning the recruits and teaching them how to handle weapons. But more than once Foster had seen that glazed look in Fontaine's eyes, as if there was some inner numbness that sometimes deadened his thoughts. It was the sun, or the desert, or the Legion, or the fighting. But it happened to men, and they turned into vegetables, or shot their commanding officers, or sometimes just walked off into the desert. *Le cafard,* they called it.

Fontaine was blinking, staring straight ahead, slumping a little as he marched by. Foster watched him and then glanced at each of the faces as the others passed. Most of them appeared to be only half-conscious. A few were staggering and stumbling; others had cracked and swollen lips and puffy hands.

He noted the rank with only three men, and then his jaw tightened as he saw only three men in the rank behind it. The gypsy was gone.

When the column had passed, Foster strode through the gate and marched to the front where Fontaine brought the men to attention. He returned the lieutenant's salute and then gazed coldly at the men. "Close the gate and see that it is locked, lieutenant."

Fontaine turned smartly to Laplanche. "Corporal! Close and lock the gate!"

Foster noted the fidgeting and anxious looks as the heavy doors swung shut. After the bolt thudded into place he stood silently for another half minute.

"Two men have failed to return from the march," he said. "Such men are of no use to the Legion. If they do not return to the fort within twenty-four hours, they will be shot. If they do return, they will be punished for separating themselves from their unit. Company, dismissed!"

"Do you think he'll come back, sir?" Triand asked an hour later.

Major Foster didn't answer for a minute, apparently giving the question some thought as he absently moved food around his plate.

After Triand brought the major's dinner, Foster had invited him to sit down and share the bottle of wine while he ate. It was not the major's usual practice, but Triand had accepted without hesitation. He knew the major was not pleased to be going to Erfoud, and he had noted the growing tension in the man through the past week.

"Yes, I think he will come back," Foster finally said. "But it would be better for the Legion if he deserted."

"How so, sir?"

"Because if he deserted we could shoot him and hang his body in the compound for a week or two so the recruits could watch the vultures feast on him."

Triand nodded. "I see, sir." Then he was surprised to see a faint smile on the major's face.

"No, sergeant, the march today did not affect my

brains. I would shoot him, of course. But I haven't yet acquired El Krim's taste for dramatic spectacles."

Triand smiled, relieved. "I'm happy to hear that, sir."

"No, the gypsy will probably come back, and if he can, he'll bring the other man. Which is too bad, because the man who fell is the kind who should never have joined the Legion. He'd be better off dying out in the desert."

Foster pushed his plate away and sat back thoughtfully studying his wineglass. "The gypsy is another problem—probably the most difficult kind we have to deal with in the Legion. In one way or another, men like that have to be broken. If they aren't, they become symbols of insubordination—thumbing their noses at authority. If they get away with it, they become heroes to all the other recruits. This means loyalties will be divided. With a man like that under his command, in a crisis, an officer can never be certain if the men will follow orders, or if they'll turn to their hero for guidance. It's a dangerous situation."

"I see your point, sir."

Foster swirled his wineglass and gazed broodingly into it for a minute. "So you can appreciate how much easier it would be if the man tried to desert and we could get rid of the problem simply by shooting him." He snorted softly. "As it is, we may have to kill him anyway."

Triand nodded and finished his wine as the major seemed to be lost in thought. Then he rose and gathered the dishes on a tray. "Monsieur Marneau has been asking to see you, major."

Foster nodded faintly. "Very well. Tell him I'll see him."

After the sergeant left, Foster gazed absently across the room, thinking about Madame Picard. Since that night when she went out with the gypsy, he had not been back to Leon's. It was bad policy for the commanding officer to be seen in such places, he had told himself. But he had since wondered if he had really stayed away because of the woman. The worse thing he could do would be to get involved with a woman like Madame Picard. Still he found himself thinking about her and wondering why she had affected him the way she had in her apartment that day.

She was one of those people in the other world that he knew nothing about and did not understand, and until now he cared little about. But for some reason her presence was like a constant shadow in his thoughts.

He finally smiled ironically to himself. Maybe it was he who was being touched by *le cafard* instead of Fontaine. He quickly finished off his wine, dismissing the matter from his mind, and went out to the balcony overlooking the compound.

Several dozen recruits were milling around below watching the closed gates, waiting hopefully for their two friends to come back.

Sometimes he wondered if it might be better to have a forty-mile march on the first day of training. You could talk to recruits all day about what would happen if they tried to desert, or slacked off in training, or dropped out of formation on a march. But it meant nothing to them until they saw the results. They never believed that the desert was cruel, and the Arabs were cruel, and the Legion had to be cruel to make men fit for survival.

Foster heard the door open and close behind him and he knew Marneau was waiting. "Major?" the man finally said.

By the tone of his voice Marneau was growing impatient. Foster turned and strode briskly into the room. "Yes, Monsieur Marneau, what is it?"

"I was under the impression, Major Foster, that we would be leaving for Erfoud by now."

"You were under the wrong impression." Foster didn't bother to look at him. He stood at the small desk and glanced through the stack of dispatches that had come in during the day.

"May I ask what is causing the delay?"

"There is no delay, monsieur. There are a hundred and eight recruits out there, most of whom have never handled a rifle before or looked an Arab warrior in the eye. I know that they are not good soldiers yet, and so does El Krim. When we go to Erfoud, I want El Krim to know it will cost him lives if he attacks the excavation."

Marneau looked only half-satisfied, but he let it pass. "I should also like to inquire about the hiring of Arab workmen, major. Lieutenant Fontaine expressed the opinion that we cannot expect the workmen to be loyal or reliable."

"Lieutenant Fontaine is correct."

"I don't understand, major."

"The men we are hiring will be loyal and reliable only as long as El Krim tells them to be so, Monsieur Marneau. It is very likely that every one of them has been handpicked by El Krim, and they will do exactly what he tells them to do."

Marneau blinked at him. "My God, man, you mean you're hiring El Krim's spies to work for us?"

Foster smiled. "If you wish, we will ask them if they are spies before we hire them."

"That's ridiculous, major."

"That is correct. However, if you would care to search Bousaada for some Arabs who are not loyal to El Krim, you certainly have my permission. But I warn you that El Krim also will be interested in your search, and if you are lucky enough to find such Arabs, they will certainly have their throats cut as quickly as their names are added to your list."

"Then, you're saying—?"

"Precisely. The only thing we can do, monsieur, is make certain that the workers we take with us have no knives or pistols." Foster smiled broadly at him. "Welcome to Morocco, Monsieur Marneau."

Marneau stared at him, then frowned. "I didn't realize—"

"Don't worry. The government and the people at the Louvre are one hundred percent behind you, monsieur. I am sure they are very concerned that you do not lose your eyes and your tongue."

The sarcasm was lost on Marneau. The only

words he heard were "government" and "the Louvre."

"Yes, yes, of course," he said and smiled. "I still don't think you appreciate the importance of what we are doing, major."

"No, I don't," Foster said flatly.

"Well, I think that once we find that tomb and you have a look at it, you'll feel differently. By the way, have you seen Madame Picard lately?"

"No, I haven't. Why?"

"I asked her to come and pick up her father's things, and she hasn't come. Do you happen to know where she lives?"

"No, I do not," Foster said quickly.

"I wonder if that gypsy fellow might know." Marneau frowned for a minute and then smiled. "Do you suppose she's having an affair with him?"

Foster felt his face redden, and he slammed the papers on the desk. "Monsieur Marneau, I am not interested in wasting time with idle gossip! If you have no further business to discuss, please excuse me!"

Marneau gaped at him for a minute and then a faint smile came to his face. "No, I have no further business, major. Good night."

Foster glared at the door after it closed. Then, with the sound of men shouting and cheering below, he looked sharply toward the balcony.

He didn't hear the pounding on the gates until he reached the balcony. Then he saw men racing across to open it.

"Keep those gates closed!" he screamed.

They stopped running and looked up hesitantly as the pounding finally stopped. Foster left the balcony and hurried down the stairs and outside. The cheering had resumed, and three steps out the door he stopped short, staring at the top of the wall.

The gypsy was on the parapet, grinning down at the recruits as he steadied himself. Then he jumped.

Foster watched silently as the man ran to the gates and heaved the bolt aside. He disappeared, then came back a few seconds later carrying the other recruit.

There was more cheering as the gypsy marched

to a position directly in front of Foster. There he eased the second man down, half-supporting him as they both came to attention and saluted.

"Two-six-eight-nine-three and two-six-eight-nine-two reporting, sir."

Foster gazed at the man, looking for a smile or the trace of a sneer. But the gypsy stared evenly back at him, the muscles of his arm quivering as he held the salute.

"On a march, we do not go back for stragglers, mister!" Foster said. "A man dies where he falls!"

"Yes, sir."

Foster glanced at the recruits, then nodded. "I am going to make sure you do not forget. Sergeant!"

Triand moved up quickly. "Sir!"

"A rope for the gypsy. The other man can go to the punishment cell."

IX

"As you can see, madame, it is truly an authentic vase of exquisite design dating from the seventh century. It was found in Mecca, very close to the tomb of the Prophet Mohammed. Conceivably, madame, it was at one time blessed by the touch of his lips."

Simone smiled as the man carefully held the small vase out to let her examine it. Dust and encrustations of old plaster covered a good part of the piece and the inside was thick with cobwebs.

She had expressed no interest in seeing such an artifact. In front of the man's booth several colorful Moroccan rugs were draped across a makeshift table and she had paused, idly touching them and admiring the colors. But as quickly as the man noted that she was European, he had gone into his act.

"I must show you something, madame," he said and glanced furtively in both directions. Then he had rummaged in a battered trunk and come up with the vase, half-hiding it as he told her how it had been in the possession of his family for thirty-seven generations. But alas, circumstances were such that he must now make a pilgrimage to Mecca, and to do so he was forced to sell the valuable piece.

"It is a very lovely vase, monsieur," Simone said, turning it in her fingertips. Having seen such sixth- and seventh-century pieces in her father's study, she couldn't help admiring the workmanship on the encrusted plaster. And no doubt the cobwebs had taken considerable time to accumulate on the inside. As to the vase itself, she suspected it was mass-produced in

Marrakesh or Fez. She handed it back and smiled. "I am afraid I am unworthy of such an honor, monsieur. The vase is no doubt priceless and should be sold to a museum."

"Truly it should, madame. But then of course my family would learn of its sale. That is why I will sell it privately, for nothing. Only two hundred francs, madame."

Simone thanked him for his generous offer and moved on past the next booth, glancing casually at the gold and silver rings and bracelets. Farther along at the side of a large open area a man was brewing mint tea over an open charcoal brazier. She bought a cup and sat down at a table under a sagging sheet.

On the open cobblestones a weathered old man was squatting down smashing empty wine bottles, shouting something in Arabic as he scattered the splintered shards around. When ten or twelve people had gathered, he straightened and made a final speech. Then he lifted the hem of his djellaba and proceeded to walk back and forth, barefooted over the glass. The spectators smiled and nodded, a few of them tossing coins. Then the man swept up the glass with a handful of hay. When that was done he brought out several slender swords and sprinkled them with flammable liquid. Then he started his spiel again, gathering a new crowd before he ignited the liquid and slid each sword down his throat.

Simone gazed absently at the performer and the surrounding people, her thoughts drifting back to that afternoon when the train stopped on the desert and that burlap covering was suddenly lifted from the wicker cage. After a week, she could finally think about it. But she knew the shock would never completely wear off. Perhaps, like the man who walked on the glass, her soul would soon be thick with calluses.

She should not have come to Morocco. Two weeks earlier, she had received the telegram informing her of Daniel's death somewhere near Montmedy!

WE REGRET TO INFORM YOU, MADAME PICARD, THAT CAPTAIN DANIEL PICARD LOST HIS LIFE ON

NOVEMBER 6, 1918 IN AN AIR BATTLE OVER MONTMEDY. CAPTAIN PICARD WAS A COURAGEOUS SOLDIER WHO GAVE HIS LIFE IN THE SERVICE OF FRANCE, AND WE ARE PROUD THAT BEFORE HIS AIRPLANE WAS DESTROYED HE WAS CREDITED WITH HAVING SHOT DOWN THREE ENEMY AIRCRAFT. YOU HAVE OUR DEEPEST SYMPATHY.

Less than a month earlier, Daniel had gotten his first twelve-hour leave in more than a year, and they had lain in each other's arms in Paris, with Daniel assuring her it would be over soon and their lives would once again be normal. Even then Simone doubted if anything in her life would ever be normal again. Working seven days a week in a hospital for three years, she had seen too many torn and mangled bodies, and she had spent too many endless nights wondering if Daniel's would be one of those they unloaded from the ambulances the next morning.

And then four days after she received the telegram the war was over and everybody was celebrating, and two days later she received the phone call. There had been an Arab attack on an excavation site in a place called Erfoud, Morocco, and it was possible that her father had been killed.

Simone had not heard from her father in more than a year, and until the letter from the Louvre she had no idea where he was. Henri Delacorte's only interest in life was art and archaeology, and Simone's only childhood recollections of him were brief glimpses of a man curled over specimens in his study, or else going out the door with a suitcase, heading for Saudi Arabia or Mesopotamia or some other place she had never heard of. Her mother had died of neglect in 1912, and her father had missed the funeral. *Dear Simone,* he had wired. *Please take care of arrangements. Hope to be back in Paris in three months. All my love.*

Then why had she come to Morocco, Simone wondered. Had she come to verify his death, or with some slim hope that he might still be alive? Was it because he was the last fragile thread connecting her to the past and some kind of hope of restoring her life?

And then she saw the broken, mutilated body, and in the ashes of her own life, it seemed as if the last tiny spark had gone out the moment Major Foster fired his pistol. She was suddenly in a void, with no past and no future.

"You should talk about it," Marco had said when he took her home. But she couldn't. She didn't know where to begin, and there seemed to be no point in it anyway. And, more important, she didn't want somebody like Marco to get himself tangled up in her life. In many ways, his daring and carefree manner, along with his reassurances, reminded her of Daniel. And, like Daniel, he would no doubt end up giving his life in the service of France.

"More tea, madame?"

Simone looked up sharply, startled from her thoughts. The man was bending forward, smiling, a small carafe in his hand. "No, thank you," she said and gathered her purse.

"Madame is feeling all right?"

"Yes, I'm fine," she told him, surprised by the question. She smiled and moved out from under the sheet, walking toward the fort, as she picked her way through the crowded bazaar again.

Was it beginning to show on her face, she wondered. She smiled ironically to herself, wondering if she should buy herself a djellaba and veil and hide herself the way the Arab women did.

From the bazaar she walked around the side of the fort where a sentry was posted at a small door. He quickly smiled and opened it for her.

"Can you tell me where I might find Monsieur Marneau's office?" she asked.

"Straight ahead, madame, to the main building and up the stairs."

She thanked him and followed the directions across a small patio.

"Ah, Madame Picard!" a man said as she entered the building. It was Monsieur Ranier, one of Marneau's assistants. "I am so sorry about your father," he said as he walked alongside her to the stairs. "It was a cruel and inhuman thing, and most shocking that you had to witness it."

Simone nodded, not knowing what to say. It seemed odd to her that after seeing her father, Marneau and his assistants still intended to go to Erfoud and reopen the excavation. She hoped none of them had wives or children.

"And how are you finding Bousaada, madame?" Ranier asked accompanying her up the stairs.

"Very warm," Simone said.

"Yes, it is very warm. However at night it gets quite chilly. You are looking for Monsieur Marneau?"

"Yes."

"This is his office right here, madame. Permit me."

He knocked softly and opened the door a few inches. "Francois—Madame Picard is here."

Simone heard a chair scrape and Marneau's excited voice. "She is here? Now? Show her in!"

Ranier opened the door and stepped aside.

"Madame Picard!" Marneau said, holding out his hand. "How good of you to come." He almost shut the door in Ranier's face. "Thank you, Jean. That will be all."

The office was almost bare except for a desk and two straight chairs. "Please sit down, madame. May I get you something? Coffee? An aperitif?"

Simone eased herself to the edge of a chair. "No, monsieur. I would rather get it over with."

Marneau was jumping around as if somebody had dropped a hot coal in his pocket. "Of course, of course, your father's belongings." He moved behind the desk and brought a small box from one of the drawers. "I'm afraid it is not much. Most of his personal possessions were at Erfoud, of course. So we can presume that—" His face reddened and he opened the box, placing it in front of her.

Simone gazed into it for a minute and then drew out a small picture of her mother. It must have been taken when she was in her early twenties, perhaps before they were married. The face showed hope and confidence and suppressed excitement. Her future was to be exciting; her husband was already a respected archaeologist and art historian. There would be fame and recognition and a wonderful social life among the Parisian intellectuals Instead, her husband went off to dig in deserts, and she stayed home to raise a daughter.

There was little else in the box—a well-worn gold pen, some business cards, a small glass paperweight that looked like a fez, and a bottle of pills.

"Your father was a good man," Marneau said gravely as Simone returned the picture to the box.

"I am sure my mother would have disagreed with you," Simone answered coldly.

"He contributed a great deal to the culture of France, madame. For that we are grateful."

Simone closed the box. "The culture of France? If he made any contribution, he did so at the cost of his life and the neglect of his family. Would you make the same sacrifice, Monsieur Marneau?"

Marneau blinked as if he had never heard of such a thing. "Why, yes, I believe so."

Simone rose and moved toward the door. "Then you are a bigger fool than my father was, Monsieur Marneau."

"But madame—what about the box? Aren't you going to take your father's things?"

Simone smiled back at him from the door. "I don't believe he would have thought me worthy of them, monsieur. Put them in the Louvre with the rest of his contributions."

She had been foolish to expect a letter, or even a note, she reflected as she moved down the stairs. Perhaps if he had survived to seventy or eighty, he might have given some thought to his family, and he might even have had some regrets about how he had spent his life. But it was probably inconceivable to him that he might not return from Erfoud, or that the Arabs might be upset over his wanting to dig up their sacred treasures. What a surprise it must have been for him. And in those last hours, while he was being carted around in a wicker basket, perhaps he had some second thoughts about how he had managed his life. But more than likely he hadn't, and that was the tragic part of it.

When she came out into the hot sun again, she paused and looked off at the corner of the compound where several dozen recruits were thrusting bayonets into stuffed bags. Off to the side Major Foster was watching, his hands behind his back, eyes narrowed, his usual stone-faced expression. Simone smiled to herself and moved away toward the big open gates. All for the glory of France.

She was almost at the gates when she saw the man lying in the dust in the middle of the compound. He was face-down, his legs and ankles pulled behind him and tied to his wrists and elbows at the small of his back. She stared at him, shocked for a minute, and then looked across at Major Foster. His back was to her now, and only a couple of the recruits glanced in her direction.

She moved hesitantly to the man, wondering as she drew closer if he was dead. His head was twisted grotesquely to the side and his mouth was open, but she couldn't tell if he was breathing. Then, as she knelt at the side, she recognized the dust-caked hair and swollen face. It was Marco.

"Oh, my God!" she breathed, and touched his cheek.

His eyes were puffed shut and his tongue was dried and swollen, filling his mouth. "Marco?"

The eyes twitched but wouldn't open, and the cracked lips quivered faintly.

Foster had left the bayonet practice and was walking toward the main building, still not glancing in her direction. She moved quickly, angling across the compound—anger suddenly bringing tears to her eyes.

"Major Foster!"

She had no idea what she was going to say to him when he stopped. But apparently he didn't hear her as he marched on into the building.

Simone turned abruptly and strode off to where the men were practicing. A lieutenant with a deep scar on his face was now standing to the side watching the recruits.

"Lieutenant," she said and marched to a position directly in front of the man, "Would you be kind enough to get me a glass of water? A large one?"

The man looked startled, then glanced off at the men. "Of course, madame. Corporal! Get the lady a glass of water. Quickly!"

After the corporal hurried off, the lieutenant gave her a concerned look. "Are you ill, madame? Perhaps you should get out of the sun."

"No, a glass of water will do fine, lieutenant, thank you."

Behind her the men were all suddenly quiet. The lieutenant gazed narrowly at her as they waited for the corporal to return. "You are the daughter of Monsieur Delacorte, are you not, madame?" There was a noticeable twitching on the side of his face where he had been wounded.

"Yes, I am, lieutenant."

"It is regrettable, madame. I was at Erfoud when the attack came."

"And you are going back?"

"Yes."

"Why?"

"I am a legionnaire, madame. It is my duty."

Simone nodded. "I see. I hope, lieutenant, that enough of your men survive the training to provide you some protection at Erfoud."

The man frowned. "I am afraid I do not understand, madame."

The corporal suddenly appeared behind her with a glass and a clay pitcher filled to the top. "Thank you, corporal," she said. She took both of them and marched away abruptly.

Would the lieutenant order her to halt? Or send someone after her when he realized what she was doing? Simone decided she didn't care as she strode rapidly toward Marco. They would have to stop her by force, and at least she would be able to throw the water from the pitcher into Marco's face.

"Madame!" the lieutenant's voice called out from behind her.

She kept walking, the pitcher gripped tightly in her hand.

"Madame!" the voice called again, harsher this time, and she heard his footsteps coming.

She knelt quickly, sloshing water into Marco's face and mouth. Then she lifted his head, cradling it in her arms as she held the pitcher to his mouth.

"Madame, the man is being punished!" the lieutenant said. She could see his boots planted in the sand, but she didn't look up.

"I think he is being murdered, lieutenant!"

"Madame, I must ask you to stop! The man is to have no water until sunset!"

"This man will die if he doesn't have water before sunset, lieutenant!" Marco's tongue was moving now, working some of the liquid into his throat. Simone looked up sharply, her anger suddenly turning to rage. "Is that what you hope will happen—to make him an example, so it will be easier for you to turn the other men into animals! When you have such little regard for life, lieutenant, you are no better than the Arabs! You are worse, because you should know better!"

The lieutenant's cheek was twitching harder than ever now, and Simone gaped at him, for a minute wondering if he was in control of himself. His face had suddenly turned scarlet, and his body was tense and trembling. She stiffened as he strode toward her, his fists clenched.

"Lieutenant!"

It was a harsh command, coming from a balcony on the side of the main building, and the lieutenant straightened, coming instantly to attention.

Major Foster was gazing calmly down at them. "Release the gypsy," he said.

"Yes, sir," the lieutenant said and quickly saluted.

When he knelt behind Marco and began untying the ropes, Simone gazed at him with amazement. He seemed to be totally in control of himself again; the twitching gone and his face no longer flushed. She had never seen anybody undergo such a quick transformation.

She put the pitcher aside and rose, watching as the ropes came off Marco's wrists and legs. But his limbs scarcely moved after they were released, and his head dropped limply in the sand.

Two recruits were hurrying over from the bayonet practice, one of them a huge man. He seemed to smile and give her a faint nod as the lieutenant stepped back and the two men lifted Marco.

"Thank you, madame," the other man whispered as he picked up the pitcher and water glass. The lieutenant touched the peak of his kepi. Then they were all marching away.

Simone took a deep breath, letting it out slowly as she watched them disappear into the barracks. She finally turned and headed for the gate, giving Foster only a glance.

"Madame!"

She stopped and looked back, seeing no anger or pleasure or relief on his face. He was like a machine, she thought to herself. In battle, in bed, or looking down from his balcony, the expression probably never changed.

"You have done what the women in the desert do," he said. "They take care of the men. I respect that."

Was it a compliment, or was there irony in the voice? She couldn't tell. "I would do it for anyone, major."

He nodded faintly, but said nothing.

"Good day, major," she said.

Marco slept. Periodically he felt his head being lifted, and through the slits of his eyes he saw Ivan squinting back at him, with Fred and Top-hat looking over the giant's shoulders. Then he tasted cool water trickling into his mouth.

The next morning he managed to get some food down and limp out for roll call. Corporal Laplanche took a hard look at him and then smiled taking extra pleasure in kicking his hands out from beneath him when the men did their pushups. Through the rest of the day the corporal stuck close, prodding, kicking, screaming at him to keep up with the others.

The side of his face was still blistered from the sun and his stretched and twisted muscles ached into the bone when Marco finally eased himself onto his bed that night.

"Marco?" Top-hat whispered in the darkness.

Marco grunted, his arm resting across his eyes.

"You know, they're trying to kill you, Marco."

Marco didn't answer. Top-hat was probably right, but at the moment it didn't seem to matter one way or the other.

"You shouldn't have come back for me, Marco. You should have left me in the desert."

Marco smiled and then caught himself as the stretching blisters stung the side of his face. "You wouldn't have liked it out there, Top-hat," he said hoarsely. "Particularly, you wouldn't have liked those Arab women when you got to their camp. I've heard they smell bad."

He heard a weary sigh from Top-hat. "I'll never be a legionnaire, Marco."

Marco grunted. The sound of snoring had already begun to fill the room.

"I didn't tell you why I really joined the Legion, Marco."

"Ummm," Marco murmured. Sleep was already creeping blissfully into his brain.

"It was a woman—a girl," Top-hat said wistfully. "A beautiful girl. Her name was Maria. Her husband had been killed at the front." He was silent for a minute and then went on. "It was the most wonderful love you can imagine. Every day, every minute, I was with her. We were happy, Marco. Even with the war going on we were happy. And then the armistice came, and we went to a grand party. I rented tails and a top hat, and she looked magnificent in a white gown. It was satin. We drank and danced and sang and the future was going to be wonderful." He paused again. "And then, while we were in bed in her apartment, the door opened and a man was standing there."

Marco was hearing only half the words. Top-hat was in bed and a man was standing in the door. "Umm," he grunted.

"It was her husband. He was not dead. He was very much alive, except he had only one leg. After struggling up three flights of stairs to surprise his wife, he just stood there looking at us. It was as if we were just one more in a long line of betrayals. You know what I said to him, Marco? I said, 'I thought you were dead.' How's that for a nice warm welcome for a returning war hero?

"He didn't say anything. He just stood over to the side and smiled sadly while I got my clothes back on. Maria had her head under the pillow, crying. When I was all dressed in my top hat and tails, I said, 'I'm sorry,' and I left. I stumbled down the stairs to the street and walked for hours. It seemed as if every wounded man I saw was staring at me, giving me the same look as Maria's husband. That's when I passed the Legion recruiting office. I didn't even hesitate."

Marco was half-asleep now, more conscious of the groaning and snoring of other recruits than what Top-hat was saying.

"Marco, I think I'd rather desert than go to Erfoud. And they're going to kill you."

"Ummm," Marco grunted.

"Will you ask Madame Picard to help us? If we don't try now, you're going to be killed by Foster or killed by the Arabs at Erfoud. Even if you're not, you're never going to see Madame Picard again. If we get away, you could meet her in Tangier or somewhere in Spain. Marco?"

Simone in Tangier. Marco pictured himself in a small candlelit restaurant with Simone smiling across the table, lifting a drink. There was no dust or sand or smells of sweat. "To freedom, Marco," she was saying, "And to you and me."

"Marco?"

"Uh-huh?"

"Will you talk to her?"

Yes, he thought sleepily, and returned to the restaurant. "To freedom, Simone. And to you and me."

It seemed like only minutes later when he was suddenly awakened. Something was pressing hard across his throat, cutting off his breath. He reached quickly to his neck, blinking into the darkness, trying to rise. But something huge was crushing his chest and stomach, pinning his other arm down. Then he felt the cold steel of the rifle barrel across his windpipe and he saw the broad shadow hovering over him.

"Don't make a sound, gypsy," a voice growled.

It was Laplanche. Marco could make out the features, and he could smell the musky sourness of wine on the man's breath. He twisted, trying to shift the pressure of the rifle from his throat to the muscles on the side of his neck. He was partly successful, and then he saw the second shadow—somebody going through his things.

"You can make it a lot easier, gypsy," Laplanche whispered. "Where are the earrings?"

Marco moved his lips but no sound came. Laplanche eased the pressure a little and brought his head closer. "Where are they?"

"I gave them to Madame Picard," Marco choked out.

"I don't think so, gypsy."

A fist drove into his stomach just under the breastbone and he gasped for air.

"Move his head," the second man hissed.

Laplanche grabbed Marco's hair and twisted to the side, quickly clamping the rifle across his throat again. Then Marco felt the hand moving under his pillow.

"Well, well, well," the second man laughed. "So you gave them to the lady, huh? In that case, you won't miss these little trinkets at all."

"Give 'em to me!" Laplanche muttered.

Marco heard a movement on the next bed, and then a shout came from Fred's thin voice, hoarse with sleep. "Hey, what's going on!"

The pressure suddenly lifted from Marco's throat and he saw the rifle butt swing across, catching Fred squarely on the chin.

"What——!"

Fred was halfway out of his bed when the blow landed. He staggered backwards, sprawling across his own cot and crashing into Ivan's.

Marco wasn't sure what happened next. As quickly as the rifle swung past his face, he was out of the cot and swinging, his fist hitting rough cloth and then hard bone—either someone's chin, or an elbow. Then he was down, tripping across Top-hat's cot and landing in the middle of the floor. When he regained his feet, the lights came on, and there was a face in front of him. He slugged the man as hard as he could, then whirled, driving his fist into another body that was half-turned away from him.

Suddenly everybody in the barracks was yelling, cursing, swinging at somebody. Bodies were crashing across cots, rifle butts were cracking against heads and ribs, the whole building exploding.

In the confusion Marco glimpsed Laplanche's face and drove a fist into his nose. Then he was twisted around, trying to dodge blows from the other direction.

He heard Lieutenant Fontaine's voice screaming from across the room, and Sergeant Girard was commanding them to come to attention. But the brawl went on. Then he saw Laplanche's body suddenly rise in the air, his arms and legs flailing. A split second later he was crashing through a window and there was Ivan grinning.

"Hit the dirt!" somebody yelled. For a second Marco paid no attention to it, then he heard the deadly chattering of a machine gun and he stared in disbelief as the windows burst from the wall and sprayed splinters of glass across the room.

"Ivan, get down!" he screamed and dove for cover.

There was dead silence when the shooting finally stopped. Marco cautiously lifted his head—enough to see that all the windows were gone. Then he peered around a legionnaire who was curled up beside him. The place looked as if a tornado had hit it. Blankets, cots, lockers and uniforms were scattered all over the floor, the whole place littered with broken glass and bodies.

"Attention!" Lieutenant Fontaine commanded from the door.

They all rose, apparently none of them hit by the machine-gun fire. The lieutenant stepped into the room and moved quickly to the side as Major Foster appeared with Sergeant Triand. The major gave them all a long look and then moved slowly through the debris. From the expression on his face it might have been an ordinary inspection, giving each man a cool look as though searching for a loose button or an unpolished boot. He finally stopped, his eyes fixed on Marco.

"What happened?"

"An accident, sir. Somebody slipped and fell out the window."

Marco didn't see it coming. He had his eyes front, fixed rigidly on the wall, then there was an explosion in his jaw and he was on his back, gaping up at Lieutenant Fontaine. The man's eyes were narrowed, his cheek twitching and his fist clenched as he glared back.

"Stand at attention, mister," Foster said quietly.

Marco rolled to his hands and knees and rose. The lieutenant hit him again before he straightened, catching him squarely on the blistered cheek, sending him sprawling once again to the floor.

Marco drew himself to his hands and knees and squinted up, waiting for the command to rise again, measuring Fontaine for the best spot to hit. But they were all silent—Foster, Triand, and Fontaine gazing down at him as if bored by the whole thing.

Foster finally turned, marching toward the door, and the other two men quickly followed. When they were gone, Marco touched his jaw and the blistered cheek and pulled himself to his feet.

"You all right, Marco?" Top-hat asked. He was holding a handkerchief under his nose, catching the flow of blood.

"Yeah, I'm okay."

The men were moving around, silently picking up cots and blankets, searching for their belongings in the debris. Ivan brushed past Marco and leaned out the window. When he straightened, he had Corporal Laplanche by the collar, dragging him back inside. He dropped him roughly on the floor and held out his hand.

Laplanche was only half-conscious, but he knew what the big Russian wanted. He fumbled in a pocket and handed over the earrings.

Ivan tossed them to Marco. Then, like a tired Russian bear going off to hibernate, he lumbered across the room and eased down on his flattened cot.

Marco followed him, picking up a blanket on the way. After he curled up under it, Top-hat was leaning close to him. "Will you talk to her, Marco?" he asked.

Marco nodded and closed his eyes.

X

"How many men have escaped from the Legion?" The cook laughed as he repeated Marco's question. "I'll tell you something, my friend. If a thousand Arabs were attacking a Legion fort and the commanding officer had only one bullet left, he would use it to kill a deserter rather than wasting it to defend himself against the Arabs. The most hated enemy of the Legion is a deserter."

Sergeant Haddad was a ferocious-looking Turk with a shaved head and a waxed moustache that stuck out four inches from his cheeks. He laughed again as he hacked at a cabbage with his big cleaver. "You know why he is the most hated?"

"Why?" Marco asked.

"Because the Arabs can kill all the legionnaires in Africa, and there will still be more recruits. There will always be thousands of men stupid enough to join the Legion. But if deserters are not caught and killed, there will no longer be a Legion. If a man thinks he has one chance in a thousand of getting away, he will try it. And if one man in a thousand is successful, every man in the Legion will go over the wall. So an officer's first duty is to protect the Legion. That means his first duty is to catch deserters."

Marco smiled and hauled another crate of cabbages to the cook's chopping block. He had been working steadily in the kitchen since he had been dragged out of bed at three in the morning. It wasn't until after lunch that he casually turned the conversation to the subject of desertion. But he had already learned a good

125

deal from Sergeant Haddad about the country around Bousaada and the ferocity of the Berber tribes to the west.

"I'll tell you something about deserters," the sergeant went on. "The biggest mistake most of them make is trying to desert while they're in a place like Bousaada. They think because there is plenty of food and water and camels, they can steal what they need, or buy it, and then head out across the desert with a good chance of making it to the coast." He laughed and shook his head. "Nine out of ten of them are standing in front of a firing squad within two hours."

"Why?"

"Because, my friend, the Arabs in places like Bousaada are very poor. A couple hundred francs is a fortune to most of them, and nothing will excite them more than to see a legionnaire sliding over the wall of a fort late at night. As quick as a deserter hits the ground outside, there'll be a dozen Arabs pounding on the commanding officer's door asking for the reward. And if a man is lucky enough to slip past the fort-watchers, there will be many Arabs happy to sell him food and water and a camel. Then, as quickly as they have the legionnaire's money, they will be knocking on the gates of the fort asking for a reward and demanding that the Legion catch the deserter and return the camel and food he has stolen."

The big man laughed. "The second mistake in trying to get away from a fort is that as quick as a man is missing, it's reported by telegraph to every legion post in Africa. Which means that every Arab and Berber will also know about it, and besides the Legion, twenty million other people will be watching every stranger that comes along. No," he said with a smile, "if a man is going to escape, there is only one place to start from. That's somewhere far out in the desert where there are no telegraph wires and where there are no Arabs watching for him to come over a wall. Then, if he can outrun the legionnaires who will be chasing after him, there is perhaps one chance in a thousand he will make it."

"You mean some place like Erfoud?" Marco asked.

The cook quit chopping and gave him a long look before he answered. "Perhaps. But out there, of course, you will probably be surrounded by two or three thousand of El Krim's butchers." He smiled and hacked into another cabbage. "And for you, gypsy, I don't think anything would make Major Foster happier than seeing you being tortured by a bunch of old hags in El Krim's camp."

Marco laughed. "There is nothing in the world I would not do to make my commanding officer happy. But you still haven't answered my question, sergeant. How many men have escaped from the Legion?"

The big Turk smiled. "You will never know, my friend. The Legion admits to none, and anybody who might have made it would be a fool to boast of it."

Marco was a good, obedient soldier in the three days that followed the riot in the barracks. He did as he was told, kept his mouth shut, and for the first time gave some serious thought to his situation.

When he jumped on that truck in Paris, he had no intention of joining the Legion; and in Marseilles, after he signed his name to the paper committing himself to five years of service, he had no intention of honoring the commitment. If he had been alert, he would have made his escape after they got off the ship in Oran. But he hadn't, and now he was in a worse situation.

So, did he grit his teeth and sweat out five years of misery? Or did he go over the wall in Bousaada and have two hours of freedom before he was shot? Or did he wait until Erfoud and try to sneak past El Krim and his butchers? Five years in the Legion meant that he would never see Simone again. And of the other two choices, taking his chances at Erfoud seemed more promising. Erfoud was farther west than Bousaada, which meant it was closer to Casablanca where he could steal a boat. There would also be no telegraph lines to inform everybody of a desertion, and if it looked as if El Krim was going to attack at any minute, Foster would not be inclined to send a lot of troops out looking for deserters. The more he thought about it, the more Marco's spirits lifted.

"At dawn tomorrow," Lieutenant Fontaine said at the end of the fourth day, "we will march to Erfoud. We will remain there for an indefinite period; as long as it takes for the archaeologists to complete their work. It is very likely that El Krim will attempt to drive us from Erfoud, and we may be under constant attack from his warriors. That is why you men have undergone these weeks of intensive training. Now you will kill Arabs, or you will be killed by Arabs.

"All recruits except those with duty assignments have permission to leave the fort tonight. Any man not present and accounted for at roll call tomorrow morning will be found and shot. Company, dismissed!"

The announcement of their departure for Erfoud had not come as a surprise. For two days they had been preparing for it; cleaning and oiling rifles, packing food and ammunition, checking the cannons and covering their muzzles for the trip. Earlier in the day, a company of camel-mounted spahis had arrived to accompany them, and the fort was bustling with activity.

Marco lagged behind and tried to bolster Tophat's spirits as they all headed through the bazaar to Leon's. "We'll make it," he told him, "As soon as we get there, we'll figure out a plan. Maybe they'll make us sentries the first night, and we can grab a couple of camels and be on our way."

Marco knew it wouldn't be that simple, but Tophat had grown more depressed than ever after Marco told him that going over the wall in Bousaada was hopeless. "I'll never make it to Erfoud," he'd said shaking his head. "You'd better figure on going alone, Marco."

So Marco had solemnly promised they would escape from Erfoud and that they would make it to Casablanca. All Top-hat had to do was hang on through the march and think about sailing into the port at Cadiz.

"Have you ever been to Madrid?" Marco asked him now. "It's beautiful, Top-hat. Just like Paris, except it's warmer in the winter."

"I'd rather go to Paris," Top-hat said glumly.

"Okay. We'll grow beards and go back to Paris."

Leon's was even more crowded than the first time they had been there. A dozen legionnaires were blocking the door, and Marco and Top-hat had to push and squeeze to get past.

"There she is," Top-hat said as quickly as they were inside. "Go talk to her and I'll play some romantic music for you."

Marco smiled and moved around the edge of the crowd as Top-hat headed for the piano. Simone now dressed in a sleek Arab caftan, was sitting with Leon at the same table as last time.

"May I join you?" Marco asked moving past Leon. He drew out a chair without waiting for an answer. "You are looking more lovely than ever, Madame Picard."

"Ah, the gypsy with the earrings," Leon said, giving him a cold look.

Simone smiled and took his hand.

"Yes, I still have the earrings, Leon. Maybe Corporal Laplanche can steal somebody else's for you."

Leon gave him an innocent smile. "I am afraid I do not follow what you are saying, monsieur."

Marco laughed. "Would madame care to dance? Perhaps we can reopen our negotiations for the earrings."

"I would be delighted, monsieur."

Top-hat had turned off the scratchy victrola and was playing what sounded like a Strauss waltz. But it was hard to hear over the legionnaires' noise. Marco edged Simone into the crowd and held her close. "Thank you for rescuing me," she laughed.

"It is small payment for throwing the water in my face the other day, madame," he said and gave her a quick kiss.

"I'm happy to see you survived."

"It was nothing. I was just sunbathing. The major thought it would be nice if I had a suntan before we left for Erfoud."

"I am afraid the major is not very happy with the results."

"What do you mean?"

"He seems to be staring at you."

Marco glanced around and finally spotted Foster at the end of the bar. He had the usual stony look on his face and he turned casually away as quickly as Marco looked at him.

"I've got to talk to you," Marco said.

"About the major?"

"The last thing I ever want to talk to you about is anything as depressing as Major Foster. I want to talk about happy things—the future. And Major Foster has no place in our future."

She drew back slightly and gave him a suspicious look. "I should think Major Foster would have a great deal to do with your future."

"Simone, let's get out of here. Let's go to your apartment."

"The night is young," she said vaguely.

Leon had left the table. Marco moved her off the dance floor and back to her chair. "What's the matter?" he asked as he refilled her champagne glass.

"Nothing," she said, avoiding his eyes.

Aside from throwing water in his face and saving his life, he wondered what she had been doing in Bousaada all this time. For someone as depressed as she had been to start with, Bousaada was about the worst place he could imagine her being stuck.

"Simone," he said, "I am going to get you some money tonight, and I want you to use it to get out of here. I want you to take the train back to Oran and then catch a boat to Malaga. From there it's a short trip up to Granada."

She was staring at him like he was crazy. "What are you talking about? Why should I go to Granada?"

"Because I'm going to meet you there. Or I can meet you in Malaga."

"I'm not sure I understand what you're saying, Marco."

"I'm saying that I am going to meet you in Malaga or Granada in about ten days. From there we can go to Greece—or England—or any place you want. Any place but France. How about America?"

"You mean you're going to desert?"

"Let's say the Legion is not too crazy about me, and I'm a little disappointed in the Legion. So I will make both of us happy by resigning my high position and giving up all the pension money I may have accumulated, and I will disappear. Then, having made the Legion happy, I will devote the rest of my time to making a lovely lady happy. I can think of no better way for a man to occupy his time."

"Don't do it, Marco."

"Don't do what? The only thing that could possibly make me happy?"

"Oh, my God," she breathed. "Marco . . ."

The piano music had stopped and Marco looked up as a burst of shouting and laughter came from the dance floor. The crowd of legionnaires was moving to the side as Top-hat was being lifted from the piano stool and half-carried toward the stairs by Andre and a young prostitute.

"Make him happy, Lola," someone yelled. "Then he'll play us some good music!"

Top-hat looked resigned, letting himself be dragged along by Andre and the girl. When they reached the stairs, he stumbled, grabbing for the banister. A second legionnaire stepped in, hoisting him over his shoulder. The crowd cheered as the man carried him up. The girl waved and smiled and the three of them disappeared.

"Will that make your friend happy?" Simone asked as the scratchy victrola started up again.

"No."

"Would it make you happy?"

He shook his head. "Top-hat and I are both thinking of the future. He wants to go to Spain, too."

She quickly turned away and picked up her champagne. "Marco, you're still wasting your time. You would be very foolish to desert the Legion for me. You can't get away, and you would not find me in Malaga or Granada."

"Where would I find you?"

She gave him a sad look and shook her head. "Don't do it, Marco. I am not what you think I am, and if you did it for me, you would regret it for the rest of your life. There is nothing I can give you."

Marco smiled and took her hand, gently turning the palm up. "I don't expect you to give me anything. Your palm tells me that you are having a very low time, that you think everything is hopeless. It also tells me that this will change abruptly and that you will be extremely happy in a very short time. I only want to be with you when that happens. Trust me."

Her eyes glistened as she drew her hand back and turned away. "Please don't do it, Marco."

A cheer suddenly came from the crowd and Marco turned to look at the stairs. The prostitute was coming down again, a weary half-smile on her face.

"Hey, that's a new record," somebody yelled, "Four minutes!"

The girl stopped and glared into the crowd as everybody cheered and clapped. "A record for nothing," she said. Then she shrugged and grinned. "He couldn't do it. He couldn't do anything."

Marco winced as he saw Top-hat coming down behind her. He was looking out at the crowd but his eyes were glazed and empty, and he moved past the girl as if she didn't exist. People were laughing, some of them yelling at him to try again. Another prostitute grabbed his arm and talked to him as he pushed through the crowd to the door. He pushed the girl away gently and walked out.

Marco quickly rose, touching Simone's arm. "Wait for me in your room."

"Marco—"

"Wait for me," he said and hurried for the door.

The patio was dark and crowded, legionnaires and prostitutes passing bottles of wine around. Marco finally spotted Top-hat trudging up a narrow street toward the fort.

"It's nothing, Top-hat," Marco said as he caught up, "Don't worry about it."

Top-hat laughed softly. "That's right, it's nothing. I am nothing. I am nothing to France, nothing to the Legion, and nothing to a prostitute. I have finally found out what I am, Marco. I should be grateful."

Marco put a hand on his shoulder and smiled as they walked. "We're all nothing, Top-hat. We all pretend to be something, and some of us believe it after a while. But it doesn't mean a thing. We'll go to Erfoud and then gallop off to Casablanca and take a boat to Spain. We'll still be nothing, but we'll have some fun doing it. Then you'll start thinking you're something again. The only piano player ever to escape from the Foreign Legion."

"I can't do it, Marco. I can't do it."

"Two weeks ago, you thought you couldn't march or carry a pack or survive one more day in the Legion. But you've done it. You'll make it to Erfoud and then to Casablanca."

The picket at the gate frowned curiously at them as they passed, and Top-hat suddenly stopped short of the barracks. "Go on back, Marco. I'm just going to go to bed."

Marco had an uneasy feeling about things. Considering the mood Top-hat was in, he could imagine him walking back through the gates and heading out across the desert. "No, I'll go in with you," Marco said.

"You should not be with legionnaires, madame," Leon said when he finally returned to the table. "Particularly with the recruits. The officers have no money, and the recruits have even less."

She had been keeping an eye on the door hoping Marco would return, but almost an hour had passed. "Then why do you permit them in your café?" she asked.

"Ah, they have no place else to go. It is a service to the Legion."

Simone smiled. "And if I do not drink with legionnaires, who is left, Leon?"

The man smiled. "Who is left? There are the three archaeologists. But I am afraid they are a bit advanced in age. I am afraid you would find them less energetic than one would hope."

Simone nodded. "And that leaves?"

"Madame," he said and lightly touched her hand. "I am a far more sophisticated man than you might suppose. I am well acquainted with Paris and Rome, and I have the means for getting there—something few others in Bousaada have."

"I'm afraid I don't know what you are talking about, Leon."

"I am talking about a way out of Morocco, madame, should you ever need one. I could accommodate you at a most reasonable fee."

"What is the fee?"

"The fee, madame, is no more than kindness and consideration on your part. I sometimes find myself lonely in such an isolated place as Bousaada."

Simone smiled. "I was under the impression I was being very kind and considerate by sharing your table with you, monsieur." She picked up her purse and rose. "And I hope my company has eased your loneliness."

Leon rose quickly to his feet and stared as she walked off.

Most of the legionnaires were drunk by now, and she had difficulty making her way through the crowd. A corporal grabbed her wrist, pulling her toward the dance floor. Simone wrenched herself free and moved quickly away, squeezing through the men. And then Francois Marneau suddenly had a firm grip on her elbow, guiding her along.

"Thank you," Simone said once they were moving through the patio.

"It is my pleasure, madame. Perhaps it would be best if I escorted you home."

He took his hand from her elbow and she smiled indifferently at him. "I'm not sure I want to go home, Monsieur Marneau."

"Then may I walk with you?"

"If you like."

Once they reached the narrow streets and the singing and shouting were behind them, she had a feeling of great relief. She turned in the general direction of the fort, uncertain of where she wanted to go.

"It's their last night in town," Marneau said. "I guess we can't blame the men for acting that way."

"It is your last night, too. Aren't you nervous about what will happen at Erfoud?"

Marneau shrugged. "Major Foster seems to be a competent officer."

"But is France a competent nation, monsieur?"

"I'm afraid I don't understand, madame."

"No doubt the officer accompanying my father to the excavation was also competent. What I am questioning is the competence of a nation that sends competent men to their deaths."

"Well—" He smiled and gave her a sidelong glance. "I don't know that we could put it that way, madame. Certainly there are risks. There are always risks in worthwhile endeavors."

"I can appreciate risking lives in order to save other lives, Monsieur Marneau. One might even justify a war on that basis. However, I cannot appreciate the idea of sending men off to battle and probably to their deaths for the sole purpose of adding another treasure to the Louvre. I particularly cannot appreciate it when that treasure is someone else's property. I see no difference between what you are doing and what a conquering army does when it invades a country and loots people's homes."

Marneau smiled and nodded. "France is a democratic nation. I am sure the decision of the government would be approved by the people."

"Unfortunately I think you are right, monsieur. It is too bad that the people of Morocco and all of those in the Arab world are not also given the opportunity to vote on the decision."

They had reached the gates to the fort and Simone stopped, gazing inside at the lighted window behind Major Foster's balcony.

"Once you have seen the sarcophagus of the Red

Angel," Marneau said, "I am sure you will feel differently, madame. And as much as you can say the treasure is the property of the Arabs or Berbers, you must
remember that it has been buried for almost three thousand years without their knowing of its location.
Probably a good many of them do not know of its
existence. I would also like to think, madame, that
your father's life was not lost in vain."

Simone looked at the man, wondering what she
was doing here and why she was even bothering to
talk to him. He was as empty and opinionated and
supercilious as her father had always been, and like her
father, there was nothing in the world that would ever
change him. A feeling of great weariness suddenly
came over her, and she didn't want to talk about it, or
think about it, or about anything else that had to do
with right or wrong and good and bad.

"Are you all right, madame?"

She smiled and nodded. "Yes, I am all right.
Thank you for accompanying me, Monsieur Marneau.
And I wish you good luck at Erfoud." She turned
quickly and walked along the wall of the fort, following the narrow path at the edge of the bazaar. She
felt tired and numbed, as if she could no longer cope
with the problems other people seemed to thrust upon
her. If Marco deserted, it would be because of her. If
Leon kidnapped her and sold her to some Berber chieftain, it would be because she had drunk his champagne
and had not been grateful enough to reciprocate by
offering her body. And no doubt Monsieur Marneau
would have an uneasy time in Erfoud because she
hadn't congratulated him for being a thief.

"I am sorry, madame," the guard said, "Do you
have a pass?"

"Major Foster is expecting me."

The man hesitated, then quickly opened the
small door and stepped aside.

There were no lights in the hallway at the top of
the stairs. In the semidarkness, she moved along to the
last door and knocked softly.

The major showed little surprise when he opened
the door.

"May I come in?" she asked.

He stepped silently to the side and she moved past.

It was a long, narrow room, partially divided to give the appearance of two rooms. Near the door was a desk and a chair and a small table, apparently serving as an office. The other room had a sofa opposite the bed, with several Moroccan rugs on the floor.

"Will you offer me a drink, major?"

"Help yourself." He nodded toward the other room.

The bottles were on a low table at the foot of the bed. She moved into the room and then stopped short, staring at the sofa.

The girl was prettier than most of the prostitutes she had seen in Bousaada. She was stretched out lazily on the cushions, partially propped on an elbow as she eyed Simone over her drink. She was dressed in a black silk caftan.

"Won't you join us, major?" Simone asked as she turned and poured herself cognac.

"No," Foster said.

She smiled, amused at her own behavior. It was what people called an awkward situation. In Paris, or anywhere else in the world, she probably would have been embarrassed and quickly excused herself. Now she almost enjoyed it.

The girl didn't appear to appreciate the humor of the situation. She glared at Simone and then muttered something to the major in Arabic. He answered with his usual indifference, and the girl glared at him. Then she emptied her drink and swung her legs to the floor.

Simone smiled. "If you would rather I left, major, I will go." But she made no move to finish her drink or go for the door.

"You are welcome to do as you please," he answered. Then he spoke to the girl in Arabic again.

Whatever he said, the girl seemed to think about it for a minute. Then she reached behind the sofa for a shawl and marched to the door, muttering all the way. The major said nothing, continuing to gaze silently across the room at Simone as the door slammed.

"Are you sure you won't have a drink with me, major?"

He shook his head.

"Do you mind if I sit down?"

The sofa was still warm where the girl had been lying. Simone smiled to herself, wondering if her body gave off as much heat, or if that was a professional talent. She rested her head back and closed her eyes.

"I suppose you find it amusing that I've come here."

"I find *you* amusing," the major said.

She looked at him, almost surprised by hearing anything more than yes or no. "Then why don't you laugh, major? Or don't you know how?" She smiled and closed her eyes again. "No, I don't suppose you do. Not a man like you."

"Madame," he said, "You know nothing about me."

"I know everything about you, major. You're the one who knows nothing."

A slight smile came to his face, but there was no humor in it. "Very well. Then you tell me something about myself."

"May I have another drink first?"

"You can have the whole bottle if you like."

He made no move and she got the bottle herself, placing it on the floor next to the sofa after she poured more into her glass.

"For one thing, major," she said, dropping her head back, "I know that you will never present me with any problems to solve. You will never force me to make any decisions, and you will never fall in love with me, or anybody else. That makes you stronger than most men."

He was still standing between the two rooms, his eyes narrowed slightly as if he found the conversation, or her, or her drinking a little distasteful.

"And the reason you are stronger, major, is because you have only one all-consuming interest in life. You are a soldier, and you will not allow yourself to be anything else. You are not a romantic soldier, or a soldier dedicated to the glorious aims of the Republic of France, or a soldier setting out to find the Holy Grail. You are simply a soldier—a soldier who does exactly what his superiors command, and that is the only thing that matters. Isn't that right, major?"

She emptied her glass and rose, smiling as she moved slowly across the room. "You know why I am here, major? Because I don't want you to kill Marco. I don't want him to love me. I want Marco to be safe, to do as he is told, and to continue living. If he no longer loves me, it will save his life. Do you understand that?"

She laughed when he didn't answer. "Of course you don't. If you did, I wouldn't be here. There is only one thing you understand, isn't there, major?"

Was she drunk? How many bottles of champagne had Leon opened? Two? Three? And had he drunk any of it? Marco had drunk a little. And now two half-tumblers full of cognac. Yes, she admitted, she was probably drunk. Probably she was totally out of control, and if somebody asked her to walk a straight line, she would be unable to find the line. She took a long, deep breath and looked the major squarely in the eye.

He was a rock; an immovable, impenetrable, solid, thousand-ton monument to duty, stability, loyalty and truth. He was the future, and let all of the sniveling, sensitive worms of the world beware. Anyone who deviates from the gospel of Major Foster will experience pain. Deep, excruciating pain. And by their cries and moans and whimpers the major will know there is success, progress, and obedience.

What had she been telling him, she asked herself. She was standing coolly and calmly in front of the great man, looking smugly up into his face, and she had forgotten what she had been talking about. It must have been pain.

"I think I am no longer affected by pain, major," she said. "And perhaps you aren't, either. But I am sure that inflicting it is your only pleasure. You do not drink because you have nothing to forget. You do not reach out for help because to do so would mean you are no longer Major Foster. And you do not love because love shows weakness and inadequacy and a desire to be whole and fulfilled. So your only pleasure can come from pain. From the pain you can inflict on others, and the pain you can feel from the emptiness of your life. You are a professional soldier, Major Foster, and I salute you. You get paid for killing, and what better circumstance can a human being have than to be rewarded for causing misery? I love you, major, because you are useful, and very few of us in the world can make such a claim. You have no feelings to interfere with being a good soldier, and thus you are the perfect tool and the most useful soldier in the world. You are useful to France, and to Monsieur Marneau, and to me, and to—"

She didn't feel the blow. It landed somewhere on the side of her face and she had no recollection of stepping back, or falling, or landing on the bed. But she was suddenly on her back and she felt a pleasantly warm sensation in her cheek as she stared up at the hard, quivering face above her.

"Hit me again, major," she said. "I love you. Take off my clothes and beat me."

She stared numbly at him as he turned away and slowly began to undress. Then she covered her eyes and wept softly.

She was not in her apartment. Marco stared at the open suitcase next to the bed and then checked the small lavatory behind the partition.

It was just as well, he told himself as he hurried back to Leon's. Maybe Leon had fed her enough champagne that she was forgetting her troubles for awhile.

Top-hat had finally gone to sleep. Marco had talked for an hour about Malaga and Granada and all the things they were going to do when they got there, and Top-hat had finally laughed and asked about the food. He didn't think he would like gazpacho, he said. Peppers and uncooked onions did not agree with him.

"Then we will cook the onions," Marco told him, "And we will smuggle French wine across the border from Bordeaux."

"Thank you, Marco," he finally said. "Without

you I never would have lasted this long. You're a saint."

"I am a gypsy."

"You're a gypsy saint," he said groggily.

Marco had smiled and pulled the blanket close to his neck. When Top-hat was finally breathing deeply, he slipped out of the barracks and headed for Simone's apartment.

He was not really surprised to find the place empty. She had told him she would not go to Malaga or Granada, and she was proving it by not going to her apartment. And to protect him she would refuse to do anything else he asked. So he would not ask her to do anything more. No matter what she said, he was going to desert in Erfoud, and he would be in Malaga in ten days, and she would have the money to get there. She had no decisions to make, and no power over his decision. No matter what she decided, he and Top-hat would be in Malaga. It was the only way to convince her.

The crowd outside Leon's had thinned considerably, and inside the legionnaires were far less energetic than when he left. Ivan and Andre were nowhere in sight, and only Fred was sitting at their table.

"Marco," he grinned happily from behind the cracked glasses, "I'd like you to meet Miss Hafid. She lives here in Bousaada."

The girl looked to be about fifteen years old, but she wasn't at all shy about where she was resting her hand. Marco smiled at her and eased into the chair next to Fred. "Have you seen Madame Picard?"

"No, I think she left about an hour after you did."

"Alone?"

Fred shrugged and shook his head. "I don't know."

Marco glanced around and felt a little relief when he saw Leon talking to the man at the cash register. Marneau and his two assistants didn't seem to be around, and neither did Foster. He wondered if Simone had deliberately disappeared. She probably had some women friends in Bousaada by now, and it wouldn't be difficult for her to find a place to stay. Marco splashed some wine into one of the dirty glasses on the table and gazed thoughtfully at Leon.

"Has Leon been around all night?" he asked Fred.

"Yes, he has. He's been watching the girls, making sure they keep busy. I had to pay him to let Miss Hafid sit at the table with me."

Marco smiled and downed the wine. "Maybe we can make Leon pay something in return. I'll see you later," he said and moved back into the shadows to the wall. He waited until Leon was moving off in the other direction and then he slipped through a back archway that led to a tiled staircase.

There was no one in sight. Corridors led away in both directions, and somewhere off in the darkness a girl was laughing. Marco stood silently for a moment, listening, then went up the stairs.

At the top there were more empty corridors. He moved off to the right toward a heavily carved door with some tiny Arabic lettering on it. Then he crouched, sliding a steel pin into the tumblers of the lock. When it clicked open, he slipped inside and quickly closed the door behind him.

He smiled, knowing he was in the right place. A huge desk flanked by fancy leather chairs stood at the far side of the room. On the other side was an over-sized couch piled high with silk-covered pillows. Only Leon would have an office like this.

Marco tried the pictures on the wall first. None of them had anything behind them. Then he checked under the rugs, moving systematically from the door to the desk. Finally, just behind the high-backed swivel chair he found it.

It was fancier than he expected, but not nearly as sophisticated as some of the safes he had seen in Cannes and Nice—and not very well hidden in the floor. Within three minutes he had made the correct turns and he felt the gentle, almost imperceptible click from the tumblers. He drew the heavy cover open and flopped it gently to the side.

There were two compartments. One was stuffed with jewelry—everything from watches and earrings to unmounted gems. Marco rummaged through the wastebasket and found a large envelope. When it was filled with jewelry, he took the bundles of cash from the other compartment and stuffed them in his pockets. Then he closed the safe and replaced the rug.

A tile roof slanted away just under the window. He stepped out and worked his way cautiously to the edge, then dropped into the alley below.

He suddenly smiled as he moved through the dark streets. It felt good to be practicing his old profession again. It was unfortunate that the task had not been more challenging. Perhaps if he returned to Bousaada someday, he could lift a few of Leon's gold teeth.

Simone was still not at home. Marco pulled back the covers of her bed and emptied the jewelry from the envelope. He left the cash under the pillow and covered everything, leaving the bed as neat as he had found it. Once he was down the stairs and through the archway he turned right, heading back to the fort.

XI

The corporal's whistle screeched like a frightened jungle animal. *"Allez-vous, allez-vous!"* he shouted and then was gone through the door.

Marco swung his legs to the floor and sat still for a minute, yawning, rubbing his face. It was still pitch-dark outside, but the two hanging lamps had been lit. Men were muttering, clearing their throats, lighting cigarettes, groping numbly for consciousness. It was the last time they would be waking up in Fort Bousaada; probably the last time they would be sleeping in a decent bed. They had thirty minutes to dress, eat breakfast, and be ready to march.

Marco twisted around to see if Top-hat was awake. Then he frowned at the bed. It was empty, the blanket neatly smoothed and tucked into the corners.

"Fred, where's Top-hat?"

Fred was carefully adjusting his glasses over his ears. He glanced at the empty cot. "I don't know. Maybe he got up early."

Marco felt his heart thump a notch faster as he frowned at the bed again. It had been a little after midnight when he got back to the barracks from Simone's apartment. Top-hat was sleeping soundly then. Going to bed so early, maybe he also woke up early and went out for a walk. Or maybe he had been called for kitchen duty. That must be it, Marco finally decided. Then he smiled, thinking about Simone and the money and jewelry he had left in her bed. She had probably found it by now.

With his towel across his shoulder, Marco trudged off to the latrine with Fred and Ivan. "How'd things turn out with Miss Hafid?" he asked.

Fred didn't look too happy. He shrugged and smiled sadly. "I was going to take her home, and Leon made me buy a bottle of cognac before he would let her go. Then she went in the bathroom for a minute. That's the last I ever saw of her."

"You mean she never came out?"

"I guess she went out some other way. After about ten minutes, I asked one of the other girls to go in and see if she was sick or something. The girl checked and said the bathroom was empty."

Marco groaned sympathetically, at the same time wishing he had done a little more than steal Leon's jewels and money. He should have locked the son-of-a-bitch in his office and set the place on fire.

He held his head under the icy faucet and then rubbed his face and hair with the towel, finally coming awake.

"Marco?" Fred said in a strange voice.

He was standing perfectly still, as if frozen in place, his eyes fixed on something at the far end of the dark room. Marco frowned and looked off into the shadows. Then his heart stopped.

It was Top-hat. From the overhead pipes, a taut rope stretched down to the knotted loop around his neck and his head was twisted grotesquely to the side. A toppled stool was lying against the wall, and Top-hat's feet were dangling less than a foot from the floor. Marco closed his eyes and took a long, slow breath.

"My God!" Fred murmured. "Poor old Top-hat."

"I can't do it, Marco. I can't do it."
The words kept echoing through Marco's head, and in the next half hour he moved in a daze, hardly conscious of what he was doing. They cut Top-hat down and laid the body out on his bed with everybody in the barracks watching in stunned silence. Then Ivan found the tails and crushed top hat he had been wearing when they first met him. He held them out, giving

Marco a questioning look. Marco nodded and Fred and Ivan dressed him, laying the top hat gently on his chest. When they were done all of the men dressed and put on their packs, then each man gave Top-hat a salute as he filed out.

The compound was teeming with activity. Mules and camels were being saddled and loaded, Arab workmen were jabbering and running around, piling their belongings on five or six scrawny donkeys, and the veteran legionnaires were straggling out of the mess hall, pulling on their packs. The recruits formed lines and stood silently while the others came into formation.

"Company, attention!" Fontaine shouted when the major came striding out.

They all lined up now: the legionnaires, the spahi cavalrymen, the Arabs standing silently behind them. Foster took a position at the front and gazed silently at them for a minute. "Report!" he finally commanded.

"Report!" Fontaine repeated.

"Number one platoon all present and accounted for, sir," a voice barked out.

A moment later Marco had his second shock of the day. Along with the two hundred other legionnaires he noticed the movement on the balcony of the major's quarters and he glanced up, thinking nothing about it. Then he caught his breath and stopped breathing, not quite believing his eyes. It was Simone.

She had come through the French doors wearing a robe, and now she was looking casually down at the men, hugging herself against the early-morning chill. Marco felt his jaw tighten, then he nodded as Ivan gently nudged his elbow.

She seemed to be making no effort to find him among the two hundred legionnaires. She gazed at the major for a minute and then looked off at the city as if she had little interest in watching the dull routine of soldiers reporting. Marco dropped his gaze and stared rigidly at the stucco wall thirty yards in front of him.

"Number four platoon all present and accounted

for, sir," a voice announced as the reports continued.

"Number five platoon," Laplanche barked out just to the left of Marco. "One man missing, sir."

Marco glanced at Foster, feeling his anger rising. The major seemed unaware of Simone's presence on the balcony behind him. He gave Laplanche a hard stare and squinted at the recruits. "Where is he?"

"The man is in the barracks, sir," Marco said before Laplanche could answer. "He is at rest."

Foster glared at him, the tone of sarcasm too strong to miss. Lieutenant Fontaine turned for the barracks, but Foster stopped him. "Stay were you are, lieutenant," he commanded, and strode off himself.

Marco squinted up at Simone while they waited. She was gazing past the troops now, apparently looking at the Arabs behind them.

There was no doubt in Marco's mind that she was deliberately avoiding his eyes, and he felt angry and sick and betrayed all at once. Why had she done it? And why was she now flaunting it—showing every man on the post that she had given herself to Foster? Or was the demonstration solely for his benefit?

Marco lowered his gaze to the wall again as Foster came marching out of the barracks. Simone was not going to look at him. She was not going to smile or wave, or do anything that would give him the slightest hope. Her message was clear and simple: she was telling him precisely what she had not had a chance to tell him the night before—that she did not love him.

Foster was holding the silk top hat as he stood with his legs spread, glaring at the recruits. "This man made a contract with the Legion," he said. "He has broken that contract. This man was not tough enough for the Legion, and there will be others among you not tough enough. For such men I can guarantee only one thing. You will either become tough enough and you will become legionnaires, or you will die."

Marco glanced at Simone and then back to Foster. Whatever pleasures the major enjoyed during the night, he was still the same son-of-a-bitch when he got out of bed this morning.

Marco winced as the silk hat suddenly hit the dust and skidded to a stop. Foster gazed coldly at the men and then turned and mounted his horse.

"Lieutenant, see that the legionnaire in the barracks is buried. In his *uniform. A vos ordres.*"

"Yes, sir," Fontaine answered with a salute. *"Compagnie! A mon commandement! A gauche! Gauche! Armes a la bretelle! En avant! Marche!"*

As they shouldered arms and marched, Marco took a final look at Simone. She was gazing back at him, but she quickly turned, looking off at Foster as the major led the column through the gates.

"Le Boudin!" Sergeant Triand commanded from the rear. The men immediately began to sing, their voices resounding from the buildings as they tramped through the dawn-chilled streets.

Marco didn't sing. He stared numbly at the canvas-skirted kepi in front of him and thought glumly about Top-hat. A detail would be stripping off his tie and tails and dressing him in his uniform by now. Within an hour they would have a hole dug, and the entire garrison would be assembled to watch him lowered into the grave. In one morning, Top-hat would be shown more respect and consideration than all of his days in the Legion.

"They're going to kill you, Marco. If we don't try now, you're going to be killed by Foster, or killed by the Arabs at Erfoud. You're never going to see Madame Picard again."

Marco smiled bitterly. Top-hat had been right about the last part. And in one way or another, Foster was doing a good job of killing him.

So there would be no candlelit table in Tangier or Malaga. And Top-hat would not be the first piano player to escape from the Foreign Legion, and Madame Picard was now the richest woman in Bousaada. And for Marco Segrain, the only remaining question seemed to be that of survival. Could a lieutenant who was half-mad and a major who was half-machine kill a half-gypsy who had escaped from every police department in Europe? Marco smiled. He didn't think so. If he had to be a soldier to survive, he would be a soldier.

And Major Foster could worry about Madame Picard from now on.

"*Pour sûr c'est un sacre copain,*" the men roared out, "*C'est ce que tous les gars disent.*"

Marco straightened his shoulders, lifted his head and joined the singing.

They came on it quickly—almost unexpectedly—and yet they knew it was coming. All through the morning of the second day they could see the vultures rising and circling and descending far ahead of them. They crossed some low, rocky hills and then tramped across mile after mile of dunes as the sun rose higher and the searing heat enveloped them. The only sounds were the monotonous thudding of boots, the grunts and rasps of dry-throated breathing, and the soft clatter of pots and pans from the loosely packed donkeys at the rear of the column.

"Company, halt!" a hoarse voice finally commanded from the front, and all the sounds suddenly stopped.

A thin flagpole was standing crookedly on a high mound of dirt, but the flag was gone. To the left of that were a dozen legionnaire tents, all of them sliced and torn and hanging in shreds. Farther to the left and extending around to the back of the excavation were shallow trenches and mounds, outlining what must have been the defensive perimeter when the attack came. It was now littered with bodies; empty-eyed skulls and skeleton hands protruding from blood-caked uniforms. A twisted machine gun was lying in a trench, the ammunition belt emptied of its cartridges.

Major Foster drew his pistol and fired across the site, sending the last of the vultures flapping heavily into the air.

"Why was the position not fortified, lieutenant?" he asked.

Fontaine didn't appear to hear him for a minute. He was sitting stiffly in the saddle, his eyes fixed on the dead bodies as if reliving the nightmare. He finally blinked at the major. "It didn't seem necessary, sir. The archaeologists . . . they were confident they could find the burial tomb very quickly. And until the last days there seemed to be no threat of attack."

"There was always the threat of an attack, lieutenant. Otherwise there would have been no point in your being here."

The side of Fontaine's face was twitching again. He nodded and glanced at the distant sand dunes as if expecting another attack at any minute. "Yes, sir."

"Have the men bury the dead. Then I want this place fortified."

Fontaine nodded. "Yes, sir."

There was little material with which to build fortifications. From the deeper parts of the excavation, a few boulders were lifted and moved to the perimeter, but there were only enough to provide cover for the cannons and the four machine guns. Trenches were dug behind a three-foot mound of earth to complete the circle. After three days of work, Foster released the Arabs and fifty of the legionnaires to go ahead with the excavation.

There was no question about their being watched. The sentries Foster posted a thousand yards out at each corner all reported seeing El Krim's men observing them and sometimes circling the excavation. At night the sentries were picketed only fifty yards out, but they too reported shadows moving close to them in the darkness.

Foster had mixed feelings about their chances of surviving an all-out attack by El Krim. If he wanted, El Krim could probably assemble two or three thousand warriors, bringing tribesmen from the mountains and distant villages into the fight. Such men would be poorly equipped, carrying only knives and swords and old muskets, but enough of them charging all at once could easily overwhelm the two hundred men defending the excavation. The cannons and machine guns would discourage them, and very likely their casualties would run 50 or 60 percent. But if they were courageous and fanatic enough they would win.

There was another possibility. If the tomb was found quickly enough—before El Krim had time to mobolize his full army—they might be able to hold him off long enough to get the Red Angel and all of Marneau's treasures back to Bousaada and carted off on the train.

And then what? In Paris, Colonel Dechamps and the minister and all the people at the Louvre would be drinking champagne and congratulating themselves. And then they would be studying their maps again, picking out likely targets for looting in Algeria and West Africa and anyplace else they thought something might be buried. And sooner or later, Major William Sherman Foster would die along with the thousands of other legionnaires.

Foster brooded over the questions, and the probabilities of what the future would bring. And he thought about Madame Simone Picard. "You have no feelings to interfere with being a good soldier," she had said to him that night, "and thus you are the perfect tool and the most useful soldier in the world. You are useful to France, and to Monsieur Marneau, and to me, and—"

The words had stung, and they had weighed heavily on him every since. *Every man is a tool,* he had told himself. *He is a tool of other people, or governments, religions, false beliefs, the whole spectrum of powers governing the world. And who is to say that one is better or worse than any other?*

Later in the night, she had laughed and told him that her father was the most successful thief the French government had ever employed. He had devoted his entire life to looting other countries, and bringing back the Red Angel of Morocco would have been his crowning achievement. But he had died in the service of his employer, which perhaps was even more noble and admirable.

Foster smiled as he ate dinner in his tent with Triand and thought about it. She was a bitter woman, but there was probably some truth in her cynicism.

He ate slowly, habitually glancing off at the horizon, looking for the silhouette of Arabs against the orange streak of sunset. The camp was quiet now. The Arab workmen had completed their evening prayers, and in the gathering darkness there was only soft conversation and occasional laughter.

"Have you ever thought of deserting the Legion, sergeant?" Foster asked quietly. He knew the question would startle Triand and he smiled as he glanced at him.

"No, sir, I can't say as I have. Except perhaps as a recruit. I think all recruits do at some time or another."

"I never did."

"That's to your credit, sir."

"Perhaps," Foster said. "But for a man to consider deserting, he has to think there's something better than the Legion somewhere else. I never thought that."

"I don't know of anything better than serving one's country, sir."

"And what or whom does our country serve, sergeant? We are useful and loyal to it. To what is *it* useful and loyal?"

Triand looked uncomfortable with the question. "Being a soldier, I've never thought to ask myself such questions, sir."

"Of course you haven't. And that is why you are a good soldier, sergeant." Foster emptied his tin cup of wine and watched the last streaks of orange slowly dissolve on the horizon. Then he gazed thoughtfully at the flickering candle on the packing crate between them.

"Madame Picard said I was a strong man because I let nothing interfere with my devotion to the Legion. That's an interesting observation, don't you think?"

"It's a high compliment, sir."

Foster snorted softly. "Perhaps. But I wonder. When a man takes orders and does exactly as he is told, he takes no responsibility for his actions. I am not so certain that requires strength."

"There is always some responsibility in carrying out orders, sir."

"Yes, but there is not the responsibility of choice. Accepting orders and carrying them out is a low level of responsibility. The choices are limited and the ramifications are slight. It would appear to me, sergeant, that a test of strength can only come when the ramifications are profound and far-reaching, and carry great risks. A man is strong when he can make such choices and take full responsibility for his actions."

Triand nodded, not too certain what the major was talking about.

"A man who deserts is making such a decision," Foster said. "Sometimes it is foolish and comes from pure desperation. Nevertheless, it's a conscious choice involving great risks and responsibilities." Foster laughed and refilled his cup. "Don't worry, sergeant," he said, "I am not contemplating desertion. For me that would not be a risky choice. It would be a simple matter for a major to ride off to Tangier and catch a ship for England."

Triand smiled. "I would still try to bring you back, sir."

"Yes, I'm sure you would. And knowing you, sergeant, you would probably be successful." Foster shook his head. "No, it's not desertion I'm thinking about, sergeant. But for the first time in my life, I'm not looking forward to going into battle. I would do anything to avoid this fight with El Krim. Sacrificing two hundred—or even ten—men to put a few gold baubles and trinkets in the Louvre is not my idea of a glorious and honorable military action. On the other hand, I can see where El Krim's sacrificing a thousand or two thousand men to save those same trinkets might be considered a glorious and honorable choice." Foster snorted and got to his feet. "Not that I think El Krim is that dedicated to saving the Red Angel or preserving the heritage of the Berber culture. But it's a good symbol for him to rally all the tribes under his leadership. That coffin is going to cost the Legion a lot more than the two hundred men camped out there."

Triand nodded and picked up the dirty plates. "Do you want coffee, sir?"

"No," Foster answered. He moved out of the tent and studied the sky for a minute. High clouds were moving in from the west, promising it would be a dark night. There might even be some showers if they were lucky.

The legionnaires were all gathered around a fire, a few of the Germans singing. Foster moved to the excavation and gazed at the series of caved-in pits and the fresh trenches Marneau had been digging in the last three days. Then he strolled over to where Marneau and his two assistants were still eating.

"Ah, good evening, major. Will you share a cup of wine with us?"

"No, thank you, Monsieur Marneau. And how did the digging go today?"

"As a matter of fact, I think it was rather promising. We've found a wall that appears to have some inscriptions on it. It might indicate we're getting close to the tomb."

"Or it might just be a wall?"

"Well, yes, that's possible, too. But I think we'll be making a lot more progress now that you've given us more men."

Foster nodded, recalling that Madame Picard's father had been digging in the same spot for almost three months without finding anything. "I hope you are right," he said and moved off to the fortified perimeter. The men at the machine gun emplacements were smoking, talking quietly in the darkness. Foster stepped over the trenches and went out to where he could see the shadow of a sentry. The man quickly came to attention and saluted.

"Any activity?" Foster asked.

"No, sir. It's been very quiet."

The sentry was a barrel-chested man with a thick German accent.

"Were you in the German army?"

"*Ja, Herr Kommandant,*" the man answered with a smile.

"What unit?"

"The Sixteenth Bavarian Reserve Infantry, *Kommandant.*"

"Belgium?"

"*Ja.*"

Foster nodded and moved on, reflecting that the war had probably ended a month early for the German. In October the British artillery had almost annihilated the Sixteenth Bavarian regiment. Then they finished the job with mustard gas. Foster wondered why a man like that joined the Legion. After two or three years at the front, had he gone home and found his wife pregnant? Or did he think there was no future for him in his defeated homeland?

He gazed out at the desert for a few minutes more and then headed back for his tent. Maybe they would be lucky, he reflected. With their artillery and machine guns and all their fortifications, maybe El Krim would have second thoughts about things.

As soon as the sun came up the next morning Foster discarded any hopes of El Krim's backing away from a battle. Foster had just finished dressing when Lieutenant Fontaine burst into his tent with a grim look on his face. One of the sentries had disappeared.

Sergeant Triand, along with four or five legionnaires, was already there when Foster hurried out to the man's position. "Attention!" Triand called out and they all snapped to.

"What happened?"

A corporal saluted. "I sent a man to relieve the guard, sir. When he came out here the man was nowhere in sight. We found this."

He handed over a kepi, and Foster noted it was almost new. "A recruit?"

"Yes, sir. A man named Hastings."

There were impressions in the sand giving the appearance of movement, or even a struggle in the area. But they could have come from the pacing of the sentry. "Is it possible this man deserted, corporal?"

Foster hadn't noticed the gypsy in the group. The man stepped forward and saluted. "If I might say so, sir, I think it is doubtful. Legionnaire Hastings was enthusiastic about the Legion. He was looking forward to standing sentry duty."

Foster gave the gypsy a hard look, wondering if the man was being sarcastic, or even trying to help a deserter.

Triand turned, speaking softly. "Hastings was the man with the cracked glasses, sir."

Foster nodded, satisfied that it was not desertion. From the training reports on the man, it appeared that the gypsy was telling the truth. "Hereafter, lieutenant, all men will stand sentry duty in pairs."

"Yes, sir."

"Sergeant, have my horse saddled. And I want twenty-four volunteers—half recruits and half veterans. Have them ready to march in twenty minutes."

"Yes, sir," Triand said and followed the major back to the tent. "Are you going to try to get the man back, sir?"

"It's probably too late for that, sergeant. But if El Krim wants a fight, I'd just as soon get it started as quickly as possible. I'm not going to sit around and let him pick off our men one by one."

XII

The Arab camp was larger than Foster had anticipated. He knew El Krim could rally several thousand men if he needed them, but he didn't expect to see more than four or five hundred already in his camp. There were at least twice that number, with a good many of the tents looking like those of mountain tribesmen.

Their approach was signaled well in advance. An hour before they reached the foothills, Foster saw the sentries observing them from miles off, and their march into the shallow canyon was lined with more Arabs watching from the higher ground on the sides. If El Krim chose not to honor their white flag, they would have little chance of fighting their way out of such a confined area.

The hundreds of tents were in a broad valley less than a mile into the foothills; the largest of the tents standing squarely in the center at the end of an open path. The Arabs lining the way were two-deep, all carrying weapons of one kind or another, some of them jeering and laughing and brandishing their rifles as the legionnaires passed.

Foster lifted his hand and reined his horse to a stop. "Company, halt!" Triand commanded.

El Krim was standing in front of his tent—the great leader, proud of his position, smiling sardonically at the visitors.

"Shalam," he said flatly.

"Shalam," Foster answered.

"So, Foster, we exchange visits like the French

bourgeoise, eh?" The Arab smiled and made a broad gesture toward the crowd. "Welcome to my home. My people greet you."

Foster hadn't noticed it at first. With the mobs of Arabs pressing in on them, he had been taking note of their number and the quality of their weapons, and then his attention had been fixed on El Krim. But with the gesture he glanced off and then stiffened as he gazed at the small clearing a hundred feet to the side of Krim's tent.

A tripod of posts was standing in the middle of the area, and the stripped body of Fred Hastings was hanging upside-down and spread-eagled over a smoldering bed of coals. The handle of his bayonet was protruding from his groin, and from the deep cuts and caked blood, there was no doubt that he was dead. Foster also had no doubts that it had been a lingering death.

Sitting around the base of the tripod, a dozen or so veiled women were nodding and giggling, pleased with their handiwork as they stared back at him.

Foster took a deep breath and turned back to El Krim. "Was that your idea?"

The Arab chuckled. "Such things happen," he said with a shrug. "One of my men became restless. It is regrettable."

Foster knew the legionnaires behind him were all staring at the body, itching for some kind of revenge. But they were in no position to do anything about it now.

"I am not intimidated," Foster said quietly. "I have come to reason with you."

El Krim nodded. "I am glad to hear it, major. My people have a great respect for reason. What is it you wish to propose?"

"That you let the French have what they want. Then let them build roads and schools for your people. Let them give you food and medicine."

El Krim's smile faded and he gazed narrowly at Foster. "Roads with French signs," he sneered. "Schools that teach French. French food. Medicine from French doctors. That is a much more subtle rape of our heritage, Foster. The price of French friendship is too high."

"Is the price too high to take your people into the twentieth century?"

The crowd murmured restlessly and El Krim spit in the dirt. "The French twentieth century?! What is so glorious about that? Your twentieth century is not yet twenty years old, and look what your civilization has brought to the world—devastation. How many of your legionnaires were killed in your great and glorious war with the Germans, Foster? Is that the kind of civilization you are promising?"

"You can stop the same devastation from coming to Morocco, El Krim. If you choose war, your country and your people will be destroyed."

"No man can foretell that. Only Allah knows what the future holds."

At the mention of Allah the crowd roared, and El Krim threw up his hands. "Allah!" he called out again, encouraging them. Suddenly the mob was alive; shouting, brandishing their arms, some of them screaming and spitting on the legionnaires. "Allah, Allah, Allah!" they shrieked.

Foster sat rigidly in his saddle, knowing that the veterans would not move, but not certain about the recruits. Then, from the frenzied mass, he saw an Arab dash to the naked legionnaire's body and pick up something from the dirt. When the man straightened, he was wearing Hastings's cracked glasses, an ugly, sneering grin on his face. He turned, prodding the dead body with a stick and then spit on it, turning back to laugh at the legionnaires. Foster gazed coldly at the man, then stiffened as the crack of a rifle sounded from somewhere behind him.

The Arab's head jerked and he was suddenly sprawled on his back, a trickle of blood running down the side from his forehead.

Foster's hand had moved unconsciously to his holstered pistol, but he held it there, watching El Krim as the wailing suddenly stopped. The Arabs were confused and uncertain for a minute, some of them lifting rifles, waiting for a command. El Krim was too surprised to issue a prompt order, and Foster quickly spurred his horse, wheeling it around and marching to the side of the legionnaires.

They were all tense, their rifle butts close to their shoulders, waiting for the Arabs to make the first move. Foster glanced over the column, his gaze moving quickly to the gypsy. There was no doubt about who fired the shot. The gypsy threw the bolt of his rifle, ejecting the spent shell, then gazed defiantly back at him.

Foster kept his voice calm. "Hold your fire," he ordered as he looked over the company again. Then he turned the horse and moved slowly to the front. "Such things happen," he said to El Krim. "One of my men became restless. It is regrettable."

A faint smile came to El Krim's face. He lifted a hand signaling his warriors to stand easy, then went on as if nothing had happened. "Tell me, Foster, how would the people of France feel if foreigners came to their country and robbed Notre Dame of its altar and precious idols? Is it that the French people think they are the only ones with religion and culture? Would they stand by and do nothing? What would you do, Foster?"

"We are not in France, El Krim."

"No, but you and your French soldiers are in Morocco. You are foreigners here, Foster, and I will do exactly as you would if the situation were reversed."

"At a very high cost to your people."

El Krim gazed silently at him and nodded. "You may love France, major," he said quietly, "but you have a deceiving mistress. The civilization you so admire and to which you give your loyalty has neither a heart nor a soul, and it uses your loyalty to perpetuate its corruption. You called me a woman, Foster. But you are worse than that. You are a willing prostitute, my friend, and you can be sure that those who sent you here speak with great pleasure and amusement about the favors you do for them. So now many of us will die for their pleasure and amusement. Good luck, my friend."

Foster gazed into the dark eyes, almost believing the man meant the good wishes. He looked around at the staring Arabs, and at the veiled women huddling by the tents. Farther back, the children were gaping at the soldiers, some of them hiding behind their mother's skirts. What had those children been told about the Red Angel of the Desert? And how much would they hate the sight of a legionnaire's uniform when they grew up?

"Good luck to you, El Krim," Foster said softly. He gave the Arab chieftain a salute and turned his horse.

"Company, about-face!" Triand shouted.

The men turned sharply as Foster moved past to the front. "Company, forward march!" Triand commanded. *"Le Boudin!"*

The column stepped out smartly, their voices strong as they burst into song. The Arabs moved back, no longer jeering as the legionnaires singing resounded through the camp. The column marched down through the canyon and into the desert, their voices seeming to grow stronger as they went.

"We could handle an attack by that many men, sir," Triand said as he joined Foster at the front of the column.

Foster nodded, squinting across the empty miles of sand in front of them. "Perhaps," he said. He suddenly felt tired. The attack was coming, probably within the next two or three days, and he had an uneasy feeling that El Krim was going to settle for nothing less than total victory this time.

"I don't think there's any doubt about it," Marneau said, "The glyphics and inscriptions seem to clearly indicate the corridor leads to a royal antechamber. If this is typical of other tombs we've found from that era, we should be within a hundred meters of the Red Angel."

It was almost dark when Marneau and one of his assistants hurried over to Foster's tent and asked him to look at what they had found. He had risen reluctantly from his cot and followed them to the excavation. Two Arabs and the other assistant were working by lantern light in the deep pit, carefully scraping dirt and clay from the walls of a narrow corridor.

"It would appear," Marneau went on, "that the corridor runs off to the east another sixty or eighty meters, and the burial chamber should be just outside your fortifications over there. So, with your permission, major, I'd like to start a new excavation out there tomorrow morning."

Foster glanced across the pit at the eight or ten Arab workmen who seemed to be listening and watching with more than usual interest. If they found the Red Angel, no doubt El Krim would hear about it within a few hours. "Whatever you wish, Monsieur Marneau."

"It's remarkable, isn't it? Delacorte worked almost three months without finding this corridor. I suppose luck plays a big part in things. But I'm sure we'll find the tomb there, major."

"You may wish you hadn't been so lucky," Foster answered as he turned away. "Sergeant," he said quietly as he passed Triand, "bring the gypsy to my tent."

Foster poured himself a cup of wine while he waited. When the man came, he peered hesitantly inside and saluted. "You sent for me, sir?"

Foster nodded, indicating a rolled blanket on the other side of his makeshift table. "Sit down."

Marco gave him a doubtful look and eased down.

"Some wine?" Foster asked. He filled a tin cup and slid it across.

"Thank you, sir."

Marco glanced curiously at the major as he took a drink. He had a good idea what the man wanted to talk about, but it surprised him that he had been called into Foster's tent for the discussion. Foster was gazing into his cup, his usual stone-face looking tired and thoughtful now.

"Shooting that Arab this morning could have jeopardized everyone in the company, mister," he said. "Why did you do it?"

Marco shrugged. "Hastings was a friend of mine."

"Everybody has friends. Everybody also has an obligation to his fellow soldiers."

"Yes, sir. But sometimes there is a conflict in the obligations. Even a dead man shouldn't have to suffer indignities like that."

"And if El Krim had killed us all, would it have been worth it?"

Marco considered the question, wondering what answer the major expected to hear. "Yes, I think it would have been worth it."

Foster looked up, a little surprised. "You were lucky."

"Probably," Marco agreed. "But a man has to count on luck once in a while."

Foster nodded and poured more wine for himself. He was not certain why he had sent for the man, or why he had asked him to have a drink with him. Such fraternization was forbidden by the Legion. But so was firing at Arabs without orders.

"That night in the Swiss embassy in Paris—you were wearing an army corporal's uniform. Were you in the Hundred and Fourth?"

Marco frowned, then laughed. With all the senior officers at that reception, he wasn't surprised to hear that Foster was one of them. "No, sir, I wasn't."

"Why were you wearing the uniform?"

"To get into the embassy. To rob the safe."

"Weren't there easier safes to rob in Paris?"

Marco smiled. "Probably. But the one in the embassy was filled with money from French politicians and war profiteers. It seemed like a more interesting treasure."

Foster gave him a cynical glance. "And you were going to give the money back to the people?"

"No, sir. We intended to keep it."

Foster couldn't help smiling. At least the man was honest. "Is that how you made your living—robbing safes?"

"No. Mostly I stole jewelry. One meets much more interesting people that way."

Foster snorted softly. "I see. Well, I'm afraid you won't have much opportunity to use your talents in the Legion."

"I expect not, sir."

Foster lifted his cup. "To Legionnaire Hastings."

"To Legionnaire Hastings," Marco answered and finished his drink.

"What is your full name, gypsy?"

"Segrain, sir. Marco Segrain."

"In the future, Segrain, you will fire only when ordered to do so. Is that understood?"

"Yes, sir."

"That will be all."

Marco rose and saluted. "Thank you, sir," he said and ducked out of the tent.

Marco smiled to himself as he walked away. Shooting the Arab who was dancing around with Fred's glasses had given him more satisfaction than anything he had done since he'd been in the Legion. After he did it, he had fully expected the whole company to be slaughtered on the spot. When that didn't happen, he expected Foster to stand him up in front of a firing squad as soon as they got back to the excavation. Instead he was treated to an extra cup of wine.

Yes, he reflected, *a man had to count on luck once in a while. And a gypsy generally got more than his fair share of it.*

Foster was at the opposite side of the camp and didn't see it happen. But he heard the voices cry out and the deadly thump of earth and rock falling. Then the Arabs were screaming and running from the main excavation to the new digging site outside the perimeter.

When he pushed his way through the crowd of wailing Arabs, Foster was shocked by the size of the pit. It was almost thirty feet deep, the smooth walls on the sides indicating it was some kind of huge chamber. Now the bottom was filled with earth and rubble and rock slabs from the caved-in ceiling.

"Are there any men buried down there?"

Marneau was on the other side of the pit, peering cautiously over the edge. "None of ours, major. But there are probably four or five Arabs." The way he said it sounded like there was no reason for alarm.

"Get some men down there!" Foster shouted to Fontaine, "Fast!"

Several Arabs were already sliding over the edge and dropping in. The others were tossing shovels down for them.

"Major?" Marneau said when he came around from the other side, "I'm sure we'll find the Red Angel's coffin down there somewhere. Can we start setting up a winch to lift it?"

"Monsieur Marneau, there are men buried in that rubble. After we get them out, we will think about your precious coffin."

"I don't think there's much chance of any of those men still being alive, major."

Foster knew the man was right, but it still irritated him. "Your Angel has been there for three thousand years, Marneau. It can wait a few more hours."

An hour later, the bodies of three Arabs were brought up the ladder. The other Arab workmen carried them off to their tents and Marneau and his assistants quickly went to work. The legionnaires set up a conveyor belt to haul out the dirt and rubble, and Lieutenant Fontaine put a squad of men on the job of constructing a winch across one corner of the pit.

Foster found himself more interested in the Arab workmen than in Marneau's digging. After the bodies were brought up, they had all left the excavation area and moved to their tents outside the perimeter of the camp. Some of them were on their hands and knees, saying their prayers and bowing to the east. The others were gathered in a tight group, apparently talking things over.

Somehow they would get a message to El Krim about what had happened. Even at the risk of being shot, one or two—or maybe all thirty of them—would try to sneak away from the camp. Or maybe they would signal El Krim's patrols with mirrors. Foster looked around the desert at his own sentries a thousand yards out. Another thousand yards beyond each of them, sitting quietly on their camels, were four of El Krim's men.

With Triand following along, Foster circled the perimeter giving the gun positions one last inspection before he returned to his tent. Then he saw the two Arabs on the west side of the camp suddenly turn their camels and gallop away.

There was no indication that the Arab workmen had made any signals. Some of them were still praying and the others were still sitting and talking, or gazing silently over at the legionnaires. But Foster had no doubt that a message was on its way to El Krim.

It was almost midnight when Triand gently shook Foster's shoulder. "Sir?"

Foster sat bolt upright, staring at the man, listening. He half-expected to hear shots, or the shrieking cries of an Arab attack. "What is it?"

"They've found it, sir—the Red Angel's coffin. Monsieur Marneau thought you would want to be told."

Foster felt relieved. He rubbed his face for a minute and nodded. "Yes. Very good, sergeant. I'll be right over."

"Are you all right, sir?"

He had been dreaming. He was back at West Point; it was late at night, and he was trying to sneak out of the barracks because Madame Picard was waiting outside for him. But he was frightened, certain he would be caught, and Paul Chase was egging him on. "You're crazy. You gonna let her sit out there in the cold all night? If you don't go, I will." Foster was just going over the fence when Triand woke him.

Foster smiled as he pulled on his boots. "I'm fine, sergeant. Are you sure they've found it?"

"Yes, sir. I saw it myself."

Foster splashed cold water in his face. "Good. Maybe we can put an end to all this nonsense. Does it look as if we can get it out fast?"

"That's hard to say, sir. I imagine it's quite heavy."

"Okay, let's go take a look."

Outside, a few lanterns were burning in the camp, and a small fire smoldered by the Arabs' tents. Foster crossed the perimeter wall and followed Triand down the ladder into the pit.

Three of the four walls had gaping holes in them now, but only the one on the left was lighted. Foster ducked through the hole and followed a short corridor, then found himself in a large room. A dozen weary legionnaires came to attention, and the three archaeologists quickly turned, all of them smiling.

"Ah, there you are, major. I thought you would want to be awakened. We just broke through that wall ten minutes ago. What do you think of our Angel?"

Foster stared across the room, a little startled by the dazzling beauty of the thing. For some reason he had expected it to be encrusted with clay and dirt and covered with dust. But there wasn't a speck on it, and the intricate scrollwork and heavy gold ornamentation glowed richly in the soft lantern-light. The top was covered with a mass of jewels, almost as if someone had poured them out of a bucket into a bed of molten gold.

"It's very impressive," Foster said.

"And look at this, major."

One of Marneau's assistants stepped to the side and smiled, indicating a chest with more jewels. Foster nodded and looked at the ceiling.

"I think we'd better get everything out of here as quickly as possible, Monsieur Marneau. Very likely this ceiling is no sturdier than the one that caved in this morning. It is also very likely that El Krim will know you have found the Red Angel before the sun comes up."

"Well, I would agree with you, major, but it is very possible there is another treasure room behind this one. I think with a few more days' work we can—"

"Monsieur Marneau, I believe the purpose of this expedition was to find the Red Angel, was it not?"

"Yes, of course, major. But as long as we are here, I see no reason why we can't spend a few more days and take back everything. It's quite possible the treasures behind that wall are worth far more than what we have found in this room. There could easily be ten times this much, major."

Foster gazed coldly at him. "My orders are quite specific, Monsieur Marneau. I was to accompany you to the excavation site at Erfoud and secure the position until you found the so-called Red Angel of the Desert. My primary duty is to assure the safety of all military personnel and civilians. With what men I could spare from their duties, I was to assist you in the excavations and in whatever work was necessary to remove the coffin from the site. Beyond that, monsieur, I have no further obligations or authority. It is my intention to carry out those orders to the letter, and do it as quickly as possible."

Marneau frowned and then smiled uneasily. "I appreciate what you are saying, major. But I am sure you are interpreting your orders in a far narrower manner than was intended. When the Red Angel was discussed, the implication was quite clear that all the treasures found with it were to be included in the recovery efforts." He chuckled softly and shrugged. "I am quite sure, major, that if you send a courier to Bousaada and wire for clarification, the matter will be resolved quickly."

"I am sorry, monsieur. I have never questioned the orders of my superiors. It is not my intention to start doing so now." Foster turned quickly to Fontaine. "Lieutenant, I want two more squads of men down here immediately. The coffin of the Red Angel is to be removed from its base and transferred as carefully as possible to the open pit where we can lift it. No further excavation work is to be done by any of the legionnaires."

"Very good, sir."

"Major?" Marneau said tightly.

"Yes, monsieur."

"Is it your intention to leave Erfoud tomorrow?"

Foster considered the question and nodded. "Yes, monsieur. If El Krim permits us to leave the site tomorrow, that is my intention."

Marneau's face was reddening with anger. "This is preposterous, major. My assistants and I are going to work through the night and gather as many things as we can. I trust," he said acidly, "that you will be kind enough to transport them to Bousaada for us."

"If we have sufficient pack animals, monsieur." Foster gave him a quick salute. "Good night."

Foster glanced off at the Arab workmen when he climbed out of the pit. He wondered if they would still be there in the morning. If not, it would probably mean an attack was imminent. "Sergeant," he said to Triand when they reached the tent, "the first thing in the morning, I want the men to start packing and getting ready for the march back to Bousaada. We will be leaving sometime around noon."

"Yes, sir."

"And be sure the Arab workmen are paid before then."

"Yes, sir. May I ask a question, sir?"

Foster gazed at him for a minute and smiled. "No, sergeant, I would rather you didn't ask a question. I am afraid I might not be able to answer it to your satisfaction."

Triand frowned, then quickly saluted. "I see, sir. Good night."

Foster poured himself some cognac before he went back to bed. Then he smiled ruefully as he reflected on what he had told Marneau. Technically he was right; he would not be disobeying orders when he loaded up the Red Angel in the morning. He might escape a firing squad on such a technicality. But for what he intended to do, there was no doubt in his mind that he would be stripped of his rank and sentenced to an indefinite stay in a punishment cell. But that was something he could think about tomorrow. "Sufficient unto the day is the evil thereof," he reflected. And there was a good chance El Krim would relieve him of any need to contemplate tomorrow's evils.

He finally emptied the cup and stretched out on his cot without bothering to take off his boots.

XIII

"Levez-vous, levez-vous!" Laplanche snarled as he moved among the tents.

Except for a faint streak of orange on the eastern horizon, it was still dark. A few fires were being started in the chilled morning air, and the Arabs were already moaning and wailing, saying their morning prayers.

Marco sat up with his blanket pulled around his shoulders and took a brief look through the tent flaps. "And a good morning to you too, corporal," he said after Laplanche passed.

"Are we surrounded by Arabs?" Andre asked with his head still under the covers.

"Yes, but Fontaine is out there beating them off with a sword."

"Good. Maybe they'll kill the son-of-a-bitch."

They heard the news as quick as they dressed and moved off to the latrine. The Red Angel had been found and they would be moving out at noon. They heard the official announcement at roll call. Half the men would be on duty guarding the perimeter while the others struck their tents and packed. At ten o'clock those on the perimeter would be relieved so they could pack. Ten men would be assigned to Sergeant Triand to assist in raising the Red Angel and preparing her for transport. Marco, Ivan, and Andre were included among the ten.

The sun was up by the time they followed Triand to the pit. Major Foster was there, standing on the far side, legs apart, gazing silently into the hole. Marco and Ivan went down the ladder with Triand, while the others stayed on top to operate the winch.

The casket was resting next to the wall, covered completely with a heavy tarp. Next to it were five or six tightly closed canvas bags.

Do the bags go too, sir?" Triand asked the major.

"Leave them down there for the present, sergeant. We'll get them later."

Ropes were lowered from the winch, and through the next hour they worked carefully, inching the heavy box up, guiding it gently so it wouldn't bang or scrape against the rough walls of the pit. The archaeologists watched while they worked, giving them unnecessary advice every inch of the way.

Once the box was above the level of the ground, planks were angled across the corner of the pit and under the casket. Then, using dowels as rollers, it was moved to safe ground.

Something strange was going on, Marco decided about halfway through the operation. It was no secret among the legionnaires that Major Foster was unhappy about being in Erfoud to help the archaeologists dig up the Red Angel. There were rumors that he had protested against the project in Paris, and that since their arrival in Morocco, he and Marneau had had several heated exchanges. But by the way Foster was acting this morning, he couldn't be more pleased with things. There was almost a smile on his face when the casket was finally out of the pit. He unwrapped part of the canvas covering and peered at it as if to make certain they had not pulled up the wrong thing. Then he stepped back and nodded.

"Do you think one camel can carry it, sergeant?" he asked.

"We can try, sir. If it's too heavy, we can rig some kind of webbing between two of them."

"All right. Get the strongest camel you can find."

Triand sent a man for the camel, and while they waited Andre moved close to the casket. "Can we look at it, sir?"

Triand looked startled and gave him an angry glance, but Foster smiled faintly. "Let them see it, sergeant."

Triand hesitated, then quickly stepped forward and undid the folds of canvas. When he pulled it back, the jewels seemed to explode in the sunlight. There were hundreds of dazzling stones, some of them as big as a man's fist. Marco moved closer and smiled, touching a huge ruby surrounded by smaller diamonds.

"Is it genuine?" Foster asked.

"I wouldn't know, sir. I am not familiar with jewels that large."

"Perhaps you practiced your trade in the wrong place," Foster said with a smile.

"Perhaps so, sir." Marco stepped back and Triand pulled the canvas into place.

The camel the man brought was gray-white and looked strong enough. When it was settled on its knees, six of the men lifted the casket and set it crosswise, just in front of the camel's hump. After it was tied, the animal staggered a little as it rose, but then stood firmly.

"It's going to be a long trip, major," Triand said. "It might be safer to rig something with two camels."

"No, I think this will do, sergeant."

"Shall we take the casket off until we're ready to go, sir?"

"No, leave it where it is." Foster gazed thoughtfully at the camel and then looked over at Marco and Ivan and Andre and the three other men who had loaded the camel. "You six men—go get your coats and sashes and your rifles and come back here immediately. Sergeant," he said, glancing at Triand, "get my horse."

"Saddled, sir?" Triand gulped.

"Saddled, sergeant."

"What the hell's going on?" Andre asked as they hurried to their tents.

"Damned if I know," Marco smiled, "Maybe we're all heading for Casablanca."

They ducked into the tent and quickly put on

their sashes and coats, then grabbed their rifles. "I'm not sure I want to go to Casablanca," Andre said.

"You have no choice. A legionnaire always obeys orders."

When they got back, Foster was on his horse, shouting down to the archaeologists in the pit.

"I shall return shortly, monsieur. Then we will help you get your treasures packed for traveling."

"We can start bringing some of them up right away, major. We've got a lot of things packed in bags now."

"There is no hurry, monsieur. I would suggest you make another search of the tombs, in case you've missed anything."

"Well—" Marneau said uncertainly.

"Sergeant," Foster said, "Have those men pull the ladder out of the pit."

"I beg your pardon, sir," Triand stammered.

Marneau looked from Foster to the ladder. "But we're going to need—"

"Pull the ladder up, sergeant!" Foster ordered.

Two legionnaires jumped forward and Triand hurried to help. They quickly pulled the ladder from the pit and set it aside.

"No one is to touch that ladder until I return," Foster said.

"Major Foster, what is the meaning of this?" Marneau shouted from the pit. "We can't get out without that ladder!"

Foster ignored him. He gave the horse a gentle nudge and rode around to a position in front of the loaded camel. "Company, attention!" he said, twisting to look back. "In file, ranks of two!"

The six men lined up behind the camel and shouldered arms. "Jesus Christ!" Andre muttered as he stepped in beside Marco.

"Major Foster!" Marneau yelled, "I demand an explanation for this!"

"Sergeant," Foster said, "Advise Lieutenant Fontaine that we expect to be back by noon. Until then he is in command."

Triand looked like he was going to faint, but he managed a salute. *"Oui, mon commandant!"*

Foster returned the salute and looked over the six men, his eyes narrowed as if assessing each of them. A half-smile came to his face as he stared at Marco. Then he straightened, his eyes front again. *"En avant!"* he commanded loudly. *"Marche!"*

Marco took a quick glance back as they stepped out. Everybody in the camp, including the Arabs, was staring at them. Triand seemed to be frozen on the spot, his mouth hanging open and his eyes wide.

"Sing!" Foster commanded over his shoulder, *"Des Marches d'Afrique!"*

Their voices were weak and hesitant at first. Then Foster boomed out the words and they all joined in, their steps picking up a notch as the singing gained volume.

Andre gave Marco a questioning frown as he sang, and Marco smiled back at him. Marco didn't think there was much doubt about their destination. They were following the same course as the day before, heading directly for the Atlas Mountains.

Marco felt like laughing as he thought about it. The night before when Foster was asking about his occupation, the major didn't seem to think much of jewel thieves. Now Foster was pulling off the biggest jewel robbery in history. At least that was how the Legion and the French government would look at it.

Foster kept them singing until they were a mile or two from the excavation. Then they marched in silence, moving at a brisk pace toward the distant mountains.

"He's crazy," Andre said. "All this time I thought Fontaine was suffering from *le cafard*. Now Foster goes completely out of his mind."

"Maybe he's going to sell the casket to El Krim," Marco laughed.

"I hope to hell the price is cheap. Otherwise I think we're going to be providing the entertainment for El Krim's wives tonight."

"Maybe the price is no attack on our camp," Marco suggested.

Andre smiled. "That sounds reasonable to me. And then what happens to Foster?"

Marco shrugged. "He either blows his own brains out, or heads for Casablanca."

Andre smiled knowingly. *"Le cafard."*

Several miles from El Krim's camp, they were picked up by four, then six, then a dozen Arab sentries. They came down out of the hills or appeared from nowhere on the desert and rode alongside the tiny column, staying two or three hundred yards to the side. Foster didn't give them a glance. He sat stiffly in the saddle, eyes front, the casket-bearing camel wobbling along behind him.

More Arabs appeared as they moved into the canyon. Some rode along on the camels, keeping their distance to the side, while others watched them pass and then hurried along behind on foot.

There was no spitting or jeering or brandishing of weapons this time. But the camp seemed larger than before. Tents were pitched to the far edges of the valley, with some now on the sides of the hills.

"Company, halt!" Foster finally commanded.

They had marched into the cleared area, within a hundred feet of El Krim's tent. He was standing silently with two aides, all three staring suspiciously at the legionnaires.

Foster maneuvered his horse around and tapped the camel with his stick. The animal shifted uncertainly and went down on its knees. "Unload it," Foster said to the legionnaires.

They marched forward, three on each side and loosened the ropes. Then they lifted the casket over the camel's head and placed it gently on the ground.

"Uncover it!" Foster ordered.

There was a gasp and then a wave of murmuring from the Arabs as the canvas was pulled off and thrown to the side. The six men marched back to their positions.

Foster straightened and saluted El Krim. "From the French," he said flatly. "A gift to your people."

El Krim didn't move. He stared at the casket as if hypnotized, then his eyes flashed with anger as he looked at Foster. "How can you make a gift of something that is already ours, Foster? You insult the people of Morocco and all the peoples of North Africa."

"In spirit, it is a gift. The French wish to honor you, El Krim."

"And what do you wish, Foster?"

"My wish is that you accept this in the spirit it is given. As a token of peace."

Marco smiled to himself as both the legionnaires and the Arabs stood silently waiting for El Krim to respond. The man had all kinds of things to say on their previous visit. Now he seemed to be at a loss for words, and not very happy about it. He finally lifted his head, his eyes still coldly regarding Foster. "I accept the return of the Red Angel of the Desert on behalf of Allah the All-Merciful, the Compassionate, and Mahomet his Prophet."

"Allah, Allah!" the crowd responded automatically. But there was no shrieking and screaming this time.

"Enshallam," Foster said and nodded. He turned his horse and moved back past the legionnaires. "Company, about-face!"

Marco took one last look at the dazzling cluster of jewels before he snapped around. It was a terrible waste, he thought. El Krim would probably put all the jewels on his own casket, and they would be buried for another three thousand years.

"En avant, marche!" Foster commanded.

As if it were a daily ritual, they didn't wait for the next command. With their first step, they were singing *"Le Boudin."*

The Arabs standing along the canyon stared at them, some of them looking puzzled, others angry. But they were all silent. When the column reached the desert, Foster angled off to the left, heading back toward the excavation.

"Now, do we all face a firing squad?" Andre muttered when they finally stopped singing, "Or do we just shoot Foster in the back and get ourselves a promotion?"

"We sing some more," Marco said, "And go on to new adventures and romance with the Legion. Didn't you read the recruiting posters?"

The excavation site no longer looked like a camp. All the tents were down, including those of the Arabs, and the legionnaires' packs were stacked against each other in scattered areas. Half the men were sitting on the mounds of dirt, waiting, and the Arabs were tying their belongings to the backs of donkeys.

Lieutenant Fontaine came across and saluted as quickly as the column reached the perimeter. "The Arabs have been paid, sir. The men are ready to march."

Foster swung off his horse. "Very good, lieutenant. Company, dismissed!" he said with a glance at the six men. Then he moved to the edge of the pit.

There was no one in sight. In the corner under the winch, rows of canvas bags were standing ready to be hoisted. Apparently the archaeologists had moved into the cooler rooms to wait for the major's return. Foster smiled and moved away. "Put the ladder back, sergeant."

Triand still looked shattered. "Yes, sir."

All of the machine guns were manned, and the legionnaires around the fortifications were standing easy, smoking and talking. Foster moved across and climbed the mound in the center of the excavation.

El Krim's sentries were gone now. To the south and east there was nothing but empty desert. Foster shaded his eyes as he studied the heat-blurred horizon to the north.

"Major Foster!" Marneau cried out as he came puffing up the slope.

"Yes, Monsieur Marneau?" Foster said, still squinting into the distance.

"Major Foster, I demand an explanation! I demand to know what you have done with the Red Angel!"

"I have returned the casket of the Red Angel to its rightful owner, monsieur." He glanced down the slope. "Sergeant, bring my glasses."

Marneau's face was red, his jaw muscles twitching. "May I ask why you have done such a thing, major?"

"I already told you, monsieur. The Red Angel is the property of the people of Africa."

"I have no choice, major, but to report this to your superior officers and to the minister."

"I would expect you to do exactly that, monsieur."

Triand brought the field glasses and Foster quickly focused them on a point to the northwest.

"Do you realize what you have done, major?" Marneau asked. "Do you realize the cost and time and all the hard work invested in this project? I have worked my entire life for this!"

Foster smiled faintly. "Then your life's work is over."

Marneau started to leave, but turned back, his voice bitter. "You said the Legion is the most disciplined army in the world, Foster. Is this an example of your discipline? Or is it an act of cowardice? Are you buying your safety with the Red Angel?"

Foster moved the glasses slowly to the left toward the base of the Atlas Mountains. If someone had accused him of cowardice two days ago, he probably would have shot him on the spot. Now it meant nothing to him. "You have a right to your opinions, Monsieur Marneau. However I doubt if my giving back the Red Angel will save your life or mine."

Marneau showed no interest in the observation. "Major, I have fourteen bags of cataloged material ready to be loaded. I would like that done, and I would like to depart for Bousaada immediately."

"I will give you men to help load the bags, and you are welcome to start for Bousaada anytime you wish, monsieur. But I am afraid you will never get there."

"Why, may I ask?"

"Because El Krim has already sent men to cut off our escape. From the size of the dust cloud, I would estimate the force to be four hundred camels.

If you look hard to the northwest, you can just make
it out."

Marneau frowned, glancing off toward the mountains. Foster smiled and moved down the slope.

"You mean to say that even after you gave El
Krim the Red Angel, he's going to attack us anyway?"
Marneau exclaimed, following after him.

"That is correct."

"My God—why?!"

Foster stopped. "Because, monsieur, El Krim
doesn't give a damn about the Red Angel. It's only a
symbol."

"A symbol of what?"

Foster smiled. "Don't you understand? It is the
ultimate indignity: a symbol of all the insults the
French have heaped on the Arabs and Berbers of Morocco and all of North Africa. If it weren't the Red
Angel, it would be those bags of jewels you want to
cart back to Paris. If it weren't those, it would be something else—anything he could use to make the people
angry and inspire them to massacre the infidel invaders. What do you think El Krim has been doing since
this excavation was reopened four months ago? He's
been spreading the word as far as he can about how
the French are trying to break into a sacred tomb and
steal the casket of a great saint. If he really wanted
the Red Angel or thought it was a sacred object, don't
you think he could have dug the thing up himself? It
would have been very easy for him to do so, and to
have taken the casket and hidden it somewhere in the
mountains."

Foster smiled thinly. "No, monsieur, there is nothing that would have pleased El Krim more than having
us try to take that casket to France. He would have
attacked the excavation, and if he were not successful
here, he would have rallied fifty thousand of his people
to attack Bousaada. Then he could have added another
hundred thousand to attack Oudja and Oran. Before it
was over, he would have had every Arab and every
tribesman in North Africa turned into a fanatic follower
rallying to slaughter the infidels and graverobbers.
That, my friend, has been El Krim's aim. And now,

with the Red Angel in his possession, we have robbed him of his symbol."

Marneau was frowning as if he still didn't understand. He glanced off at the desert. "But he's going to attack anyway!"

"Of course he is going to attack, monsieur. He has to. He has to save face, and he has to justify gathering so many tribes together. What reasons he will now give his people, I don't know—that we have desecrated the tomb, or that we have taken more treasures and sacred objects than we left. You can be sure El Krim has already thought of something. And you can be sure he is angry over my delivering the Red Angel to his camp."

"Then—for God's sake—why did you give it to him?"

Foster gave him a cold look. "I have already told you that, monsieur. And, as I said, it will not save our lives. But it will probably save thousands of other people's lives. In the end, it may save France."

"Then I take it you regard this as a suicide mission, major? All these men are to be sacrificed for what you deem to be a greater good?"

"If you wish to put it that way."

"I don't think you have a right to make such a decision."

Foster smiled and slowly shook his head. "Monsieur Marneau, the decision making this a suicide mission was made weeks ago in Paris, and you concurred enthusiastically. I am merely making the best of it. If I am going to die, monsieur, I prefer to do it serving some worthwhile purpose. Now I would suggest that you ask Sergeant Girard for a rifle and spend what little time you have left familiarizing yourself with it. There is even the remote possibility, monsieur, that some of us will survive." Foster gave him a casual salute and walked away.

"There seems to be Arab activity to the northwest, sir," Fontaine said falling into step with him. "Do you think El Krim is going to attack?"

"Yes," Foster answered, "Have the men stand ready."

"Aren't we leaving for Bousaada, sir?"

"No, we are not, lieutenant. We have fortifications here and we will make use of them."

"Some of the men, sir—those who went to El Krim's camp yesterday—they said there were several thousand warriors there. They said a great many of them seemed to have new rifles."

Foster gave the lieutenant a sharp glance. He hadn't paid much attention to Fontaine lately. He looked tired and his face was twitching. "They were exaggerating, lieutenant."

"Yes, sir. I suspected that might be the case. I'll tell the men to stand alert."

The cook was ladling out the last of the soup to the six men who had just returned. Foster walked over and got the scrapings from the pot.

"Sorry, sir," the cook said, "I can fix something else for you."

"Never mind, sergeant. This is the best part anyway."

He sat on a crate and watched Fontaine while he ate the soup. The lieutenant was moving around the perimeter, talking to the sergeants, gesturing to the northwest. The men nodded, some of them picking up rifles. Others snuffed out cigarettes and stepped up on the mounds of sand to take a better look.

Foster remembered the first battle he was in and the eagerness with which he had looked forward to it. There were seven or eight hundred Tuareg warriors charging the thirty or forty men in Paperrine. But things were different then. The Tuaregs had only a few old muskets to go along with their swords and lances, so it was more like a military exercise than a battle. Even with the old Lebel rifles the legionnaires had, a ratio of fifteen-to-one didn't give the Arabs much chance. Now more than half of El Krim's men had guns, a fair number of them as good as the legionnaires' weapons. In the future, now that the war in Europe was over, there would probably be many more modern weapons being offered for sale.

The camp was quiet now, most of the men squinting out at the desert. Another cloud seemed to be rising to the west. Foster studied it for a minute after he finished his soup. Then he moved absently over to the excavation. The gypsy and the five other men were sitting in a shallow depression, talking casually.

"Segrain," Foster said.

The gypsy rose and came over. "Yes, sir."

Foster moved a few steps away, out of earshot from the others. "A man could still get through to Bousaada," he said looking off at the dust clouds. "El Krim has men waiting to stop any large movement to the north, but a clever man riding a good camel could easily avoid them. Once the battle starts, they won't bother with a lone rider."

"I'm not sure what you're talking about, sir," Marco said.

"I'm talking about a clever gypsy. And I'm thinking about a woman in Bousaada who needs you."

Marco stared at the major, not quite believing it. "The lady in Bousaada, sir—I don't think I'm the one she's waiting for."

"I didn't say she was waiting for you, I said she needs you. You are the only one who can show her there's something worthwhile in life."

Marco gazed silently at the hard, expressionless face, then shook his head. "I don't think I could leave now, sir."

"I could order you to go. Normal procedure is for me to send a message to Bousaada advising that we are about to be attacked. I have every reason to send the man I think has the best chance of getting through."

"I—I would refuse the order, sir."

Foster smiled faintly and glanced at him. "Then I would have to shoot you."

"I'm aware of that, sir."

Foster nodded. "In that case, I don't think it would be wise for me to issue the order."

"Very well, sir."

"That will be all, gypsy."

"Thank you, sir. And good luck."

Foster watched him return to his comrades and then looked off at the horizon again. The gypsy would make a good legionnaire, he reflected. Probably the best of the lot—except that his career in the Legion was likely to end within a few hours.

He moved away from the excavation wishing his tent hadn't been taken down. It would be several hours before El Krim got all his warriors organized, and some kind of battle plan formulated. Those few hours would be a good time to take a nap. Foster smiled to himself as he moved around the perimeter, making a casual inspection.

Now was the time when the men started thinking about death, and wondering why they had joined the Legion. They would think back on all the chances they might have had to escape, and wonder why they hadn't taken them. They would think about Paris and Vienna and Berlin, and about their unfaithful wives and soon-to-be-orphaned children. It was the time when they would decide that life was precious, and that they didn't want to lose it. And that would make them better soldiers than they realized they were.

XIV

They came directly from the west, the sun slightly to the left and quarter-high. A half-mile-wide dust cloud began to rise almost imperceptibly from the flat surface of the desert. But as yet there was nothing visible beneath it.

The first attack would be one of brute force: a mass of men storming forward in an attempt to over-run the legionnaires' position by the sheer weight of numbers. If the line could be broken and enough men could penetrate the perimeter the battle would be won with the first stroke. Once the legionnaires had to leave their positions and became entangled in hand-to-hand fighting, the advantage of fortifications and superior weapons would be lost. Then they would be no match for the overwhelming mass of Arabs.

Foster had anticipated the single-front attack. Of the two hundred men, he had moved all but fifty to the west perimeter. Both of the cannons and three of the machine guns were also positioned for the attack. The remaining fifty men and one machine gun were placed under Lieutenant Fontaine's command and positioned to guard the rear. During the charge, some of the Arabs would veer off and pass the excavation. It would be Fontaine's responsibility to prevent their infiltration of the rear.

What it came down to, Foster reflected as he watched through his glasses, was the question of how many Arabs would be fanatic enough to continue charging into the barrage of rifle, machine gun, and artillery fire. With a man's comrades dropping on all

185

sides, it was a hard thing to do, and if one out of ten of them faltered and panicked and turned back, the resulting chaos and confusion was usually enough to break the momentum of the attack. Then it depended on their leaders. That was always the critical point in a battle when maximum pressure had to be applied. While the enemy leaders screamed and threatened, driving their men forward, all the firepower available had to be used to convince the Arab warriors that to obey their commanders meant certain death.

Through the field glasses, Foster could now make out the broad line of mounted Arabs leading the huge army. They were still several miles away, moving slowly, allowing the foot soldiers to keep up as they approached close enough to begin the charge. Foster scanned the line, estimating that about three hundred men were riding in front. Behind them there were probably another six or eight hundred mounted warriors. As for the men on foot, it would be hard to say. Maybe fifteen hundred.

Foster lowered the glasses and looked behind him. Lieutenant Fontaine was pacing restlessly along the rear perimeter, and the men appeared to be ready. Foster glanced across to the piles of dirt in the excavation and smiled. Just behind the crest of one of the higher mounds, Marneau and his two assistants were staring off at the dust cloud, each of them with a rifle. They looked tense, their dreams of marching into Paris with truckloads of treasures no doubt far from their minds now.

"Two thousand yards, sir!" Triand called out from Foster's right.

"Artillery ready?" Foster shouted.

"Ready, sir," a corporal at each of the cannon emplacements answered.

"Set range at twelve hundred years and stand alert!"

The corporals acknowledged and Foster raised his glasses again. The mounted Arabs were clearly visible now. They were still moving slowly, the men on the flanks now angling in to make a more compact group.

"Fifteen hundred yards, sir!" Triand called.

The Arabs came slowly forward for another two or three minutes and then stopped. They were waiting for all the men on foot to catch up.

"Thirteen hundred yards."

Foster scanned the line again. Then he saw a man's arm lift, hoisting a rifle high over his head. Then they were moving.

It took three or four seconds for the sound to reach them. Then it came like a dim babble; a mixture of shouts and screams and cries to Allah.

"Artillery, commence firing!" Foster commanded.

The earth jumped and the roar of the two cannons shattered the air as they fired almost simultaneously.

"Continuous fire!" Foster commanded as he saw the first shells erupt in front of the charging Arabs. They were about fifty yards apart and well placed. Eight or ten camels and horses went down, their riders plummeting into the sand. But the gaps were quickly filled, making the line solid again. The distant pop of Arab rifles was now audible.

"Rifles and machine guns, continuous fire!" Foster shouted.

Thirty or forty of the front-line Arabs dropped with the initial volley. Others tripped and stumbled over the fallen men and animals. The losses seemed insignificant. They were now less than five hundred yards away and still coming. The roar of rifles, machine guns, and cannons was now continuous and deafening, almost drowning out the fierce screams of the Arabs.

Legionnaires were also being hit. Foster saw one of the machine gunners fall backwards, his face a splattering of blood. Another man quickly took his place, the gun idle for no more than two seconds.

The number of mounted Arabs was thinner now, probably a quarter of them down, and more falling steadily. The men on foot were a hundred yards behind; a solid mass of running bodies, djellabas flying, all of them screaming, brandishing their weapons over their heads.

The next thirty seconds would tell. Foster drew

his pistol, watching, waiting for the mass of charging animals to divide.

They were two hundred yards away, then a hundred and fifty, then a hundred, dozens of them dropping, their animals sprawling on the dunes. Foster raised his pistol, ready to fire at the first one coming over the embankment. Then he felt a small wave of relief. The mass of Arabs was splitting, most of them angling off, choosing not to ride directly into the withering barrage ahead. Only about thirty were holding their course.

Half of those went down quickly, and a few more veered away. For the others it was hopeless, but they kept coming, two, four, then eight of them swept from their saddles by the storm of bullets. Three of them made it; two men on horseback and another on a camel. They came galloping up the last dune and hurdled the barrier, the men screaming, one of them swinging a sword, the other two firing almost point-blank at the legionnaires. As quickly as their animals landed inside the perimeter, the riders were torn to pieces by twenty or thirty legionnaires turning from their positions and firing almost simultaneously.

The other mounted Arabs were now scattering to the sides, some of them jumping from their animals to fire from the cover of dunes. Others had galloped on past the excavation and were regrouping to attack the rear.

For the men on the west perimeter, the problem was now the mass of Arabs charging on foot. They were still a hundred yards off, and they were much easier targets than the fast-moving camels and horses. Foster glanced to the rear and saw Fontaine standing silently behind his men. Apparently he had given no orders for them to fire yet. Foster watched for a minute, then moved to the perimeter and picked up the rifle of a fallen legionnaire.

Under the raking fire of the machine guns, the Arab foot soldiers were dropping by the dozens, but there were at least fifteen hundred of them still coming. Foster wedged himself against the sand barrier and aimed and fired six times, seeing six men drop in front of his sights. Then he rose and moved to higher ground.

They were less than fifty yards away now and still coming. Then Foster noticed the first break. The flank to the left of the mob was faltering; a few of the Arabs stopping, then heading back or diving for cover. Foster moved quickly to one of the machine guns. "Concentrate fire on the left!" he commanded. The man swung the gun across, spraying a mass of bullets into the hesitant mass. An Arab horseman galloped forward, screaming at his men, and Foster lifted his rifle, firing quickly into the man's chest.

That did it. The entire flank of the Arab mob was now heading back, colliding with those attempting to go forward. Suddenly the whole crowd was in a state of confusion.

"Rapid fire!" Foster commanded, moving along behind the men.

Marco felt a drop of perspiration trickle coldly down his ribs as he watched the Arabs regroup a quarter of a mile beyond the east perimeter. He had yet to fire a shot. With the whole world exploding on the west perimeter behind them, all fifty of the men under Fontaine's command had remained tensely in place, waiting for the first command.

Horses and camels galloped past on both sides, their riders firing wildly as they went. They were within range, and along with the other men, Marco had sighted on one and then another of them, waiting for Fontaine's order. But the lieutenant was silent.

"Christ, we could have killed a hundred of them already!" Andre muttered. "What the hell's he waiting for?"

It was Fontaine's behavior rather than the Arabs that was giving Marco an uneasy feeling. Maybe it was a good military tactic, and Fontaine figured the recruits would waste bullets firing at the fast-moving Arabs. But Fontaine had an odd look on his face. He was standing ten yards behind the line, his hands behind him, staring rigidly out at the desert. The twitch was going, and he was blinking steadily, as if having trouble focusing his eyes. At the far end of the line, Corporal Laplanche was frowning across at the lieutenant.

"Here they come," Andre said quietly, and Marco turned back.

There were two or three hundred of them moving forward now, starting to gallop. Marco wedged himself into the embankment and picked a man with a black beard and a striped djellaba, fixing his sight squarely in the center of the man's chest.

They were less than two hundred yards away and coming fast, the screams and battle cries growing louder. Marco eased more pressure on the trigger of his rifle and waited. He held himself tense through the next three seconds and then he turned sharply and looked at Fontaine again.

The lieutenant looked exactly the same. He was blinking, squeezing his eyelids together, then frowning slightly. He looked like a man staring out at an empty sea, trying to determine if there might be a tiny ship on the horizon. Marco gaped at him, knowing the order to fire would never come. He scrambled quickly to his feet.

"Fire!" he screamed, "Machine guns, continuous firing!"

The guns exploded along the entire perimeter, the machine gun chattering on without pause.

The command had come far too late to break the attack. Camels and horses were going down and Arabs were crashing to the ground. But the momentum was still on their side.

"First and third platoons, fix bayonets!" Marco commanded. He quickly fixed his own blade as the first of the Arabs leaped over the embankment.

There were thirty or forty of them inside the perimeter now, wheeling their camels and horses, hacking at the bayonet-charging legionnaires. Marco shot one man and lunged at another, then yanked a third from his horse as the man swung himself off balance. Then Fontaine was suddenly staggering through the chaos waving his pistol. "Retreat!" he screamed hysterically, "Abandon positions! Company, retreat!"

There were less than a dozen Arabs still fighting

inside the perimeter and the machine gun was turning back those outside. Marco drove the butt of his rifle into Fontaine's jaw and sent him sprawling to the ground. Then he whirled, firing point-blank into the face of another Arab rider.

"Hold positions!" he shouted as the last of the Arabs inside the perimeter kicked at their mounts, attempting to get back over the barrier.

"Rapid fire!" he commanded as the main body of Arabs began to move off.

Two minutes later, Major Foster gazed across the excavation, watching as Lieutenant Fontaine came unsteadily to his feet. The lieutenant appeared to be dazed, staggering slightly as he moved to a high mound and eased himself down again. Foster watched him for a minute and then turned away.

He had seen what happened—the Arab charge, and the gypsy finally giving the order to fire, and then Fontaine screaming for retreat. By then Foster was moving across, calling for the machine gun on the north perimeter to swing around and give them help. But the situation was suddenly under control and the Arabs were fleeing.

The Arabs were almost out of range on both perimeters now and Foster stepped up on a mound. "Cease fire!" he called out.

Seventy-eight legionnaires were dead or dying. Another forty or fifty were wounded. Probably a thousand or more of the Arabs were dead or dying. The bodies of horses, camels and Arabs were strewn across a half-mile area on both sides of the excavation. Some of them were moving, attempting to crawl or limp away, while others moaned and whimpered and called for help from Allah. The rest of the Arabs had moved off and regrouped a mile to the north. They would attack at least once more before sunset.

Foster had the wounded moved into trenches of the excavation. The dead men were all propped into positions around the perimeter, their rifles pointing out at the desert as if they were ready and waiting for the next attack. When that was done, Foster walked over to where Lieutenant Fontaine was still sitting on the mound.

"What happened, lieutenant?"

Fontaine's head jerked up and he blinked at Foster. Then he came quickly to his feet and saluted. "One of the men, sir. The gypsy. He fired without orders, and he struck an officer." Fontaine's face was twitching, suddenly growing red with anger. "I recommend severe punishment, sir."

"When did you plan to have the men start firing, lieutenant?"

"As quickly as the Arabs charged, sir. They were regrouping beyond the east perimeter when the gypsy commanded the men to fire. Then the men did not respond to my order calling for a retreat. We were hopelessly outnumbered, sir. I have ordered the machine gun destroyed."

Foster gazed silently at the man. Fontaine was breathing heavily, the arteries of his neck pulsing at twice normal speed.

"We will have to travel by night, sir," Fontaine suddenly said. "We should take all the water we can carry and try to make it to Bousaada. They have taken the two archaeologists. I should have given them weapons."

"Sit down, lieutenant," Foster said quietly.

"There's no time, sir. We—" He suddenly looked around and frowned, as if seeing all the live legionnaires for the first time. Dazedly, he eased himself down and dropped his head on his arms.

Foster moved away, glancing at the sun. There were about two hours of daylight left. The next attack would come within the hour.

Marneau and one of his assistants were helping bandage the wounded. The other assistant was dead. Foster stepped over to a machine gun emplacement where the gypsy was sitting with the big Russian.

"Would you still disobey if I ordered you to Bousaada, gypsy?"

"Yes, sir," the man answered promptly.

Foster nodded and looked at the Russian. "How do you like the Legion, soldier?"

A big grin came to the man's face and he nodded.

"The next time, they'll be coming at us from all sides at once. They'll try to spread us out as thin as they can. How's the ammunition holding out?"

Marco smiled. "I think we have enough to kill about two thousand Arabs, sir."

"Good. Don't waste any." Foster suddenly smiled. "Do you think two thousand Arabs have a chance against a couple of first-class jewel thieves?"

Marco grinned. "No, sir, I don't."

Foster turned to go, but then stiffened as the report from a pistol suddenly cracked through the silence. Every man on the perimeter swung sharply around, rifles ready.

Lieutenant Fontaine's body was lying back against the dirt mound, his revolver still clutched tightly in his hand. Foster stared at him and then glanced at two recruits. "Prop that man's body on the perimeter and put a rifle in his hands."

They came forty-five minutes later, this time forming a broad circle around the excavation site before they charged. The maneuver drastically reduced the efficiency of the cannons. Where they shot into a mass of attackers before, they now had no more than a thin line for a target. And with the men spread evenly around the perimeter, they could not effectively concentrate their fire on any large segment of the attackers.

The Arabs formed their circle, and when they were ready a signal shot was fired. Then the shrieking and wailing began, and they were coming from all directions.

They beat off the first assault. The Arabs charged from all sides, closing the ring, giving each man the responsibility of facing fifteen or twenty shrieking fanatics coming at them across the dunes.

The south perimeter finally broke, and the attackers poured in, threatening to neutralize the legionnaires' firepower and reduce the battle to a hand-to-hand conflict between a thousand sword-wielding Arabs and less than a hundred desperate men.

Marco and Ivan and Andre were still on the east perimeter, firing as fast as they could throw the bolts of their rifles and pull the triggers. Suddenly, the Arabs were coming in behind them, galloping along the trenches, swinging their swords and firing at close range.

Ivan quickly vaulted from the trench, leaving his rifle behind, flailing his bayonet in his hand, slashing and bludgeoning, yanking men from their saddles and slamming them to the ground. Marco followed, dodging the swords, firing his rifle at faces and chests and backs, and plunging his bayonet into anything close to Ivan.

He glimpsed Major Foster up on the high mound aiming and firing his pistol, at the same time shouting off to the machine gunners, directing their fire to the charging Arabs, and then to those circling inside the perimeter. A minute later an Arab leaped from his camel and Marco crashed to the ground, the weight of the huge man knocking his breath out and sending his rifle flying off into the sand. Marco twisted, pushing at the man, grabbing for anything he could find, and then he had the man's throat in his fingers. He squeezed with all his strength, bringing his knee up hard into the man's groin, and then he was on top, driving his fist again and again into the bearded face.

When he rose, Marco looked quickly around and then grabbed up his rifle, ready for his next opponent. It took him a couple of seconds to realize what was happening. He saw Ivan chasing after a running Arab, and another legionnaire kneeling and firing at the same man. Then he saw the horses racing out of the excavation, their riders' heads bent low over the animals' necks as they fled.

There was only one machine gun firing now. Arabs were galloping away in all directions, while those on foot were scrambling over dunes, diving behind the crests to escape the last of the legionnaires' bullets. There was sporadic fire for a few minutes more, and finally there was silence. The battle was over.

Marco moved to a pile of sand and sat down, resting his head on his arm while he tried to catch his breath. He felt a hand on his shoulder.

It was Ivan. The big man looked at him and then walked back to the trenches. He lifted Andre's limp body and laid it out on the sand. Then he sat down and wiped a sleeve across his brow, looking off at the other bodies.

Marco followed his gaze, unconsciously counting the few men still alive. There were ten, maybe twelve of them. Some were coming wearily out of trenches, others lying back on the embankments.

Marco rose and walked slowly to the mound in the center of the excavation, knowing what he was going to find. At the top, Major Foster's body was lying face-down, his pistol clutched in his hand. Marco removed the gun and gently rolled him over. There were two bullet holes in the chest, and the major's sightless eyes seemed to be searching the sky, trying to find something in the gathering darkness.

"He was a good man," a choked voice said.

Marco looked up. The archaeologist was standing on the other side of the major, a rifle hanging loosely from his hand.

Marco closed the major's eyes and crossed his hands over his chest. Then he gazed silently at him, feeling his throat tighten. "Yes, he was a good man." He pulled himself slowly to his feet and saluted.

From somewhere in the excavation Marco heard the click of a rifle bolt being thrown and he saw the archaeologist staring past him. He turned and looked out at the desert.

About fifty Arabs were approaching the perimeter, their horses and camels coming slowly along behind El Krim's. Marco stared at them, knowing there was no point in trying to do anything about it.

Ivan was still sitting by Andre, squinting indifferently at the Arabs. The ten or twelve other legionnaires were standing by the trenches, their rifles held loosely at their sides.

El Krim stopped his horse at the bottom of the mound and gazed up at Marco for a minute. Then he dismounted and came slowly up the side. When he reached the top, he looked at Foster for what seemed like several minutes. Then his eyes closed and he took a long breath. "I am sorry, old friend. You tried to bring peace to our desert. May you find it in the hands of Allah."

XV

The train from Oran and Oujda had arrived late, and it was being loaded quickly, preparing to head north again in twenty minutes. Arab workmen were moving along the side oiling the wheels and washing the windows while the engine hissed and throbbed, ready to head out across the desert again.

Simone stayed close to the station house under the narrow strip of shade, waiting patiently for the conductor to announce the passengers could board.

A group of legionnaire recruits had poured out of the cattle cars ten minutes earlier, and they were gathering their equipment and helping to unload boxes of weapons and ammunition from a freight car. Simone watched them, idly studying the faces and listening to the laughter, wondering which of them would become officers, or deserters, or merely names on a dusty list recording those who had died in Morocco for the glory of France.

She had not seen Marco. Earlier that morning, Leon had come to her apartment and told her that Marco turned down the offer of safe passage to Tangier. Apparently he had been surprised and then amused by the proposal.

"I told him, madame, that it was your idea, and that you had paid in full for safe delivery of himself and one other person to Tangier, or any other Mediterranean port of his choosing. He—how shall I say—he found the proposal somewhat bizarre."

"Did he inquire who the other person might be?" Simone had asked.

"No, madame. He did not seem interested."

Simone had smiled at the irony. The "other person" might have been another legionnaire, or herself. She had no hopes or fears one way or the other when she instructed Leon what to say. But if he had chosen her, she would have gone.

Even more ironic was the "paid in full" part of the arrangement. When she heard that the Red Angel had been found, and that the legionnaires would soon be returning to Bousaada, she had taken all the jewelry and cash Marco had left in her bed and offered it to Leon as payment for helping Marco escape from the Legion. But her bargaining position had been promptly reduced to nothing. Leon had smiled and quietly confiscated the jewels and money. It was his property; he was extremely grateful for its return, and if madame was truly intent on helping the gypsy escape from the Legion, he was certain that arrangements could be made. It would require only a small consideration on madame's part, and he was certain she would not find it unpleasant.

Simone had found it unpleasant. She had watched the man dance around his room pouring champagne while he told of his travels and conquests, and then she had submitted. Three days later, the fourteen legionnaires had returned from Erfoud, and she had been surprised by the relief she felt over hearing that Marco had been one of the survivors. And then Leon was at her door, explaining that the gypsy had shown no interest in going to Tangier.

She had laughed when he finished telling her about it. Leon was embarrassed and apologetic, almost as if he had cheated her, and for the first time in his life he was not proud of having struck a profitable bargain. So she had taken advantage of the opportunity, asking him to get her a travel permit and a ticket on the train that would be leaving in two hours, and he was back at her door in forty-five minutes with all the necessary papers. Then he sadly kissed her hand and ran out to get a boy to carry her luggage to the station.

"Madame Picard! How nice to see you. Are you catching the train to Oran?" Francois Marneau was setting his bag down next to hers, consulting his watch.

"Yes, I am, monsieur."

"I couldn't be more delighted, madame. I think they are ready for us to board now. May I take your bag?"

"Thank you," she said and glanced off at the legionnaires.

A corporal was getting the recruits in formation now, shouting at them to straighten their lines. She gave them a final look and followed after Marneau as he headed for the railroad car.

"Madame?"

The voice came from behind her and Simone stopped short, quickly turning.

"Marco—" she said softly.

He took her hand and gently kissed it. Then he placed the earrings in her palm.

"They brought me good luck, Simone. Keep them. They'll do the same for you."

He held her hand, gazing into her eyes for a minute, then he quickly smiled and looked back at her palm. "I see happiness. Depend on it. Perhaps we will meet again someday."

He turned and quickly strode away, to where the recruits were now standing at attention. Simone watched as he stopped in front of the men and silently looked them over.

"You men have made a contract with the Legion," he said brusquely. "You will honor that contract. Some of you will try to quit, others will try to run away—"

"Madame!" Marneau called from the door of the railroad car, "The train is leaving shortly."

Simone nodded and moved slowly toward the train.

ABOUT THE NOVELIZER

ROBERT WEVERKA was born in Los Angeles and educated at the University of Southern California, where he majored in economics. His other novels include: *Griff, Search, The Sting, Moonrock, The Widowed Master, One Minute to Eternity, Apple's Way, The Waltons,* and *I Love My Wife.* He and his family currently live in Idyllwild, California.

ABOUT THE DIRECTOR

Diverted from an early ambition to become an actor, DICK RICHARDS became an award-winning photo-journalist and producer/director of television commercials. His extensive period research on cowboys for a soup commercial led to the idea for his first motion picture, *The Culpepper Cattle Company* in 1972. He followed this initial success with *Rafferty and the Gold Dust Twins* and the highly acclaimed *Farewell, My Lovely.*

ABOUT THE SCREENWRITER

DAVID Z. GOODMAN first worked with Dick Richards on *Farewell, My Lovely,* for which he wrote the screenplay. A major motion picture and television writer, his other credits include the screenplays for *Straw Dogs* and *Logan's Run.*

DON'T MISS
THESE CURRENT
Bantam Bestsellers

☐	DR. ATKINS DIET REVOLUTION	(11001—$2.25)
☐	HOW TO SPEAK SOUTHERN Mitchell & Rawls	(10970—$1.25)
☐	BLACK SUNDAY Thomas Harris	(10940—$2.25)
☐	DOLORES Jacqueline Susann	(10500—$1.95)
☐	THE LAST CHANCE DIET Dr. Robert Linn	(10490—$1.95)
☐	THE DEEP Peter Benchley	(10422—$2.25)
☐	VOTE FOR LOVE Barbara Cartland	(10341—$1.50)
☐	MAVREEN Claire Lorrimer	(10208—$1.95)
☐	LETTERS HOME Sylvia Plath	(10202—$2.50)
☐	THE GUINNESS BOOK OF WORLD RECORDS 15th Ed. McWhirters	(10166—$2.25)
☐	DUBAI Robin Moore	(10099—$1.95)
☐	LIFE AFTER LIFE Raymond Moody, Jr.	(10080—$1.95)
☐	DORIS DAY: HER OWN STORY A. E. Hotchner	(2888—$1.95)
☐	LINDA GOODMAN'S SUN SIGNS	(2777—$1.95)
☐	RAGTIME E. L. Doctorow	(2600—$2.25)
☐	THE EAGLE HAS LANDED Jack Higgins	(2500—$1.95)
☐	ASPEN Burt Hirschfeld	(2491—$1.95)
☐	THE MAGIC OF FINDHORN Paul Hawken	(2463—$2.25)
☐	THE MONEYCHANGERS Arthur Hailey	(2300—$1.95)
☐	HELTER SKELTER Vincent Bugliosi	(2222—$1.95)

Buy them at your local bookstore or use this handy coupon for ordering: